DESERT TALES

ALSO BY MELISSA MARR

Wicked Lovely

Ink Exchange

Fragile Eternity

Radiant Shadows

Darkest Mercy

Wicked Lovely: Desert Tales

(Art by Xian Nu Studio)

Volume 1: Sanctuary

Volume 2: Challenge

Volume 3: Resolve

Faery Tales & Nightmares

Carnival of Souls

Graveminder

The Arrivals

HARPER

An Imprint of HarperCollins*Publishers*

Desert Tales: A Wicked Lovely Novel

 For information address HarperCollins Children's Books, a division of HarperCollins Publishers, 10 East 53rd Street, New York, NY 10022.
www.epicreads.com

ISBN 978-0-06-228756-4

Typography by Ray Shappell

13 14 15 16 17 LP/RRDC 10 9 8 7 6 5 4 3 2

❖

First Edition

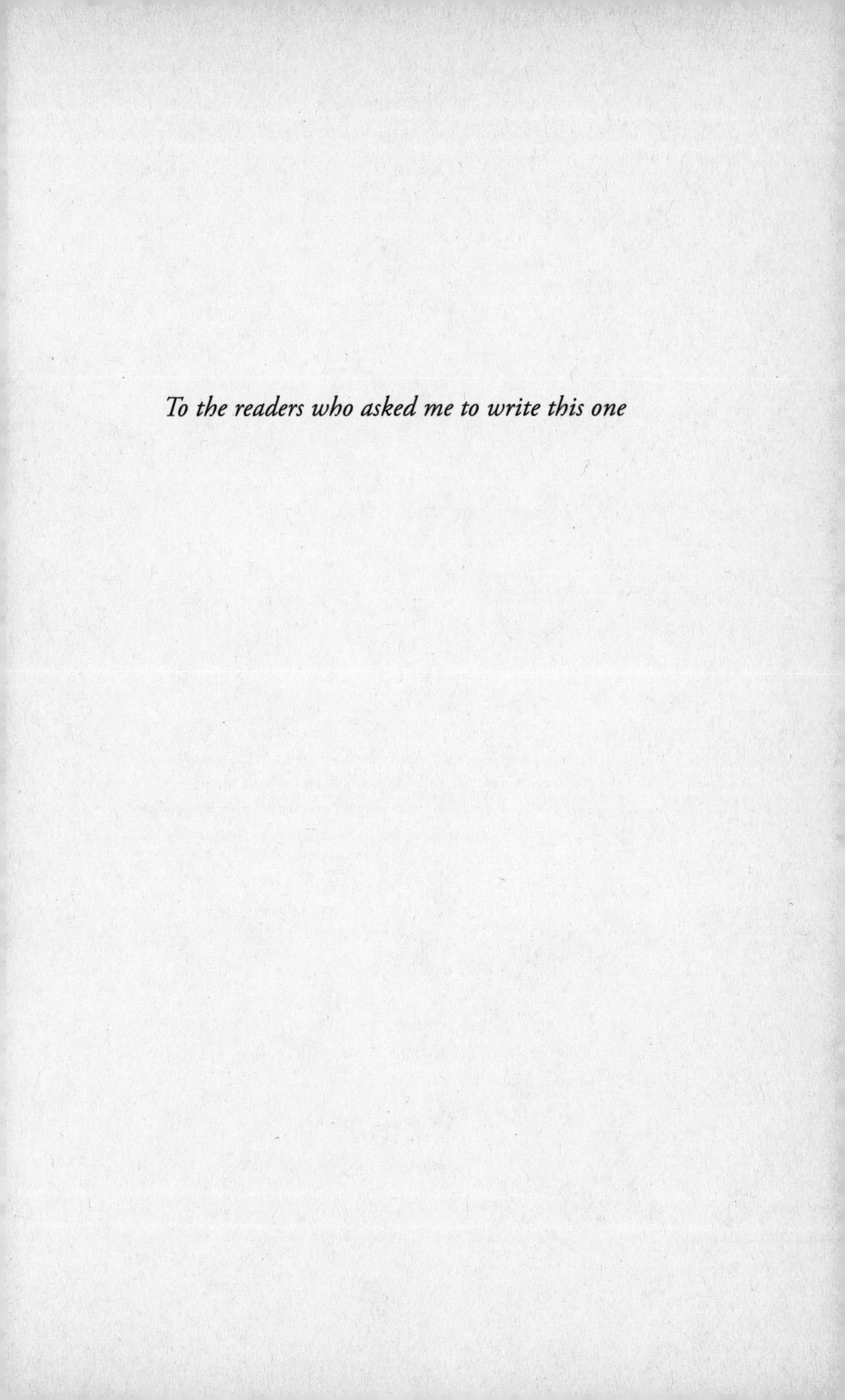

To the readers who asked me to write this one

Author's Note

Please note that this is a companion story to the original five Wicked Lovely novels. The overarching plot of the series stands on its own without *Desert Tales.* Much like the Wicked Lovely series short stories, *Desert Tales* is intended to be "extra content."

This story began while I was writing *Fragile Eternity.* I started pondering the Winter Girls and Keenan's past relationships with them. I also knew that Keenan was going to be absent in *Radiant Shadows,* and I started thinking about where he went. When I ponder, I write. In this case, to figure out what was happening elsewhere outside the courts, I wrote the three-volume *Wicked Lovely: Desert Tales* manga.

However, I also try to listen to reader requests when possible. When readers said they wanted the Wicked Lovely stories all in one place together, we released *Faery Tales & Nightmares,* a collection that included five Wicked Lovely short stories and a handful of other folklore-rooted stories. Likewise, when readers asked to read the story of *Desert Tales* without reading it as manga, I decided that not only was that a great idea but that if I were going to do it, I'd go further and expand on the story. It's been fun for me to revisit the Wicked Lovely world; I hope you enjoy it too.

With thanks for your support,
Melissa

Prologue

As she took—and failed—the test to become the missing Summer Queen, Rika's mortality ended. She stared at him from snow-filled eyes, icicles tipping her fingernails, frost clouds rising from her lips. She'd thought she loved him; worse, she'd believed *he* loved *her*. As the cold filled her, Keenan didn't touch her. He simply turned away.

The next time they spoke, he told her that he'd found the girl who might be queen, another mortal who had no idea what he was, the one who could be what she wasn't. It wasn't difficult at all to tell girls that Keenan wasn't to be trusted, and it wasn't as hard as she'd expected to convince that girl not to take the test.

Again and again, she met the girls who were not the one. Again and again, she tried to convince them not to trust him—and she succeeded.

Years passed, and all Rika had for comfort was the wolf who first came to her when she was filled with ice. No faery offered her friendship, not even those she'd spared from the fate she endured. The loneliness weighed her down almost as much as the ice that crackled across her skin, yet time and again, she stood in front of another mortal girl who refused to lift the staff. Each time, Rika was torn between the sharp satisfaction of seeing Keenan falter and desperate sorrow that her own tenure carrying the ice would continue.

Until Donia . . .

Despite all of Rika's warnings, Donia decided that Keenan was worth the risk. The color drained from her as her mortality was replaced, as she failed the test. For the first time in years, the tears that slid down Rika's face were not frozen. Water slipped over her skin instead of ice while Donia's pale blond hair became white, her body bowed under the pain, and her lips turned blue from the cold.

Rika's freedom was gained only by another's loss.

Donia fell heavily to the ground, and Rika couldn't even touch her to help her to stand. Sasha, the wolf, went to the new Winter Girl. He was hers now, like the pain and the ice. Rika felt a burst of guilt as she wished she could keep the wolf, that someone would choose to stay with her.

Rika glared at Keenan as he stood there glowing and then turned away from Donia as he had once turned from her. He had destroyed both of their lives, yet he offered comfort to neither girl. One of the faeries who advised him came to Rika, explaining her new future, treating her with all the barely hidden disdain she'd come to expect of them after she'd convinced girl after girl not to trust the Summer King.

She was no longer ice-filled, but she couldn't go back to the life she'd left behind. Everyone she'd known was dead. Rika was a faery with no family, no friends, no court; she was untethered, just as alone as she had been for the past decades. Now, however, she no longer even had a purpose.

So she'd fled to somewhere hot, hoping to burn away the memories of the ice that had lived inside her skin. When she arrived, faeries so different than any she knew in the Summer Court or Winter Court watched her, but she'd turned away from them, pretended that they were no different than the landscape around them, and they'd let her—at least, she'd thought they did.

They never acknowledged her until one night when she watched the Alpha, Sionnach, dance in the wide-open desert under a full moon. It wasn't the first or even the fifth time she'd watched him, but this time, he looked at her and grinned. Late that night, he came to her cave and was the first to talk to her. For years, he was the only one who visited her, who teased her. He didn't force her to join the faeries here, but he was her friend—her only friend.

Until Jayce . . .

Chapter 1

Trusting Keenan had been the mistake that informed Rika's entire life, a mistake that had cost her both her humanity and her happiness. She'd given everything—her mortality, her family, her health—but it wasn't enough. *She* wasn't enough.

So when she'd escaped to the desert and hidden herself away from both humanity and faeries, she'd kept to herself. It was a quiet life, but she was happy—until she met Jayce. Admittedly, *met* might not be the right way to describe her encounters with the mortal boy, but it was as close of a word as she knew, and as close as she'd come to a relationship in a very long time. She spent countless hours at his side talking to him or simply enjoying their shared silence. Jayce, of course, hadn't known how much time they'd spent together because Rika remained invisible during all of it. She might not have been *born* a faery, but she followed the rules: faeries weren't to carelessly reveal themselves to mortals.

Today, as she had so many other times since she'd first discovered Jayce staring into the sky with a bemused smile on his face, Rika was enjoying one of their art dates. She cherished her days with Jayce. Unlike the faery king she'd thought lovely when she was a mortal, the human boy she'd fallen for was the kind of beautiful that faeries couldn't be. Jayce had thick dreadlocks that were such a dark brown that they were only a shade shy of black—except for the few that were dyed purple. Today, the dreads were pulled back in a ponytail, but a few had escaped and fallen over his shoulder as he sketched.

Oblivious to her as always, he perched on a rock, sketchbook on his knee, bottle of water at his feet. Pencils, charcoal, and other art paraphernalia jutted out of his satchel and spilled onto the ground next to him, but he was lost in the moment. His attention drifted between the desert and his paper.

Rika shaded her portrait of him while he captured the desert landscape with his colored pencils. "Another perfect date," she said.

Jayce looked up, but not at her words. Like most mortals, he couldn't see or hear the fey. Fortunately, her invisibility also meant that he'd never reject her, never tell her that she wasn't the girl for him. Unfortunately, it also meant that he would never reach out and draw her closer. Still, she'd decided almost a year ago that their relationship was better if he didn't know she existed.

She followed his gaze to where a desert tortoise plodded

across the ground. When Jayce saw it at the edge of the road, he dropped his sketch pad on top of his satchel and picked up the tortoise.

He carefully lowered the tortoise onto the sand on the other side of the road. "Too many dangers for you out here." Jayce watched the tortoise continue its journey into the desert. Then he glanced at the darkening sky. "Looks like it's time for me to go too."

As he packed up his art supplies, Rika packed hers as well, but when she looked in the same direction Jayce had, her happiness fled. What appeared to be an ordinary storm to Jayce was something Rika saw as far worse: a faery raced toward her in the heart of a swirling dust devil. Surrounded by twisting sand was the source of all of her greatest sorrows, Keenan, the Summer King himself.

Embarrassingly, even in the midst of the waves of ugly emotion his presence elicited, Rika couldn't stop the sigh that escaped her at the sight of Keenan. When she'd fallen for him, Keenan had still been a bound king, the strength of summer hidden from him inside a mortal girl. Even then, he was captivating. Now that his curse was broken, he was devastating to see.

He'd spent nine centuries seeking his Summer Queen, romancing innocent after innocent. At one point, he'd convinced Rika that she was the one he needed. Worse still, he'd convinced Rika that *she* loved him enough to risk finding out if she was the one he needed. She hadn't been the missing queen, and as a result of the curse, she'd been transformed into a faery, filled with ice and cold as punishment for failing the test. Such was the horrible cost of trying to break the curse that bound summer.

Many years and many foolish girls later, the Summer King had found his mortal—a girl named Aislinn—and taken her humanity as he had all of the others. This time, the newly fey girl was filled with sunlight, and Keenan was finally radiant with the summer strength he'd been seeking for so long. To herself, Rika could admit that she was happy that the curse was un-made. A world slowly freezing would have eventually killed every living creature except for those faeries who were a part of the Winter Court. It had been a horrible curse, a horrible fate for the world.

But I still can't forgive him. Not for the loss of my mortality. Not for the trickery. Not for the years of carrying ice in my skin.

Spirals of wind and sand whipped out around Keenan as he stopped in front of her.

"Why?" Rika asked.

"Why what?" Keenan had stilled, but the air around him hadn't. The sand was uplifted, held aloft by his magic.

It wasn't really a question she could explain—or one he could ever answer to her satisfaction. Rika's words were careful, whether out of sorrow or anger she couldn't say. "Why do you still bother me?"

He paused, and in a moment, Keenan had willed the sand into two chairs. Rika wouldn't admit it aloud, but the chairs were beautiful: they appeared as solid as sandstone cliffs, like rocks with striations. The sand-formed chairs were positioned at slight angles to each other, as if they were at a small two-person table in a bistro, not in the vast expanse of desert. The Summer King wasn't quite posturing, but like every court faery he was clearly aware of his appearance. He always had been, even when half of his power was hidden away from him. Now that he was freed, he was positively preening. He sat upon a chair that hadn't existed until he willed it and waited, looking like the king he was, expecting her to be flattered by his attention and awed by his skills.

She wasn't flattered. His attention never boded well. So Rika didn't sit. Instead, she folded her arms over her chest and glared at him.

He frowned. "Is it truly such a chore to talk to me?"

"I think it is," she said. Fairies couldn't lie—that rule was as old as the cliffs that stretched out in the distance of the desert—but they could prevaricate or temper their words. Rika stepped farther away from him.

"Even now?" Keenan asked. Heat radiated from him, to him, as if his skin was breathing the extreme temperature in and out. He was the Summer King as he had only ever been in the moments when mortal girl after mortal girl risked everything for him. Now that he was unbound, he would be fully himself all the time, but the memories of seeing him like this pushed against her as fiercely as the heat.

When Rika didn't answer, he added, "You're free of the ice."

"I still dream of it." Rika turned to face him even though she knew she still looked vulnerable. "I wake up convinced that winter is still inside my veins. What you did—"

"*I* didn't do that to you." Keenan's voice filled with frustration and the heat around them flared momentarily stronger. "I didn't want you to suffer. I never wanted *any* of you to suffer."

"Did you choose me?" Rika asked softly, tilting her head so that her short hair, cut in a modern way she knew he hated, brushed her shoulder. She moved so he could see the silver jewelry piercing her ear. She was not going to live in the past, not going to look like the girl who was foolish enough to trust him. When he didn't reply, she added, "Did you convince me that you loved me?"

"I did, but—"

"Did I carry ice in my body for years because of that mistake?" She stepped closer. "Because I believed you loved me?"

"Yes, but—"

"So why *wouldn't* it bother me to see you?" She moved so close that she was in his space. He could crush her without any effort, incinerate her with the sunlight he carried inside of him, but she didn't care. She'd decided many years ago that she would never bow before him. All she had left was her pride. He'd taken everything else, and when she hadn't been the girl with sunlight inside of her, he'd rejected her.

Keenan ran his hand through his hair in a familiar gesture of frustration. The strands shimmered like glistening copper, like solidified sunlight, captivating even now. He couldn't argue without lying, but he wanted her to bend.

Rika couldn't. In the desert, the passive were less free. Maybe it had been the same in the faery courts and in the human world. Back then, however, she didn't know how important it was to speak for what she believed. She'd learned though. "Look at where we are. Cities are poisonous to me, Keenan. *Iron*, *steel*, they leave me sick now. . . ."

Despite her still-raw anger, the Summer King didn't flinch. "That's part of being faery. Almost all faeries have that limitation. It's not—"

"—fair, Keenan," she finished. "It's not *fair*."

She turned her back to him and sat in one of the sand chairs.

"It's not *unusual*," he corrected. "I was going to say it's not *unusual*. Faeries are weakened by steel and iron. It's just the way we always have been."

"But *I* wasn't always like this. I was *human* before you."

"A long time ago." He reached out as if he'd touch her. He didn't, but a sand-filled breeze that looked ever-so-slightly like fingertips brushed her cheek. "I can't take it back, but I'm sorry you're sad. I *did* love you."

"That was a long time ago too. And look where it left me. . . ."

Keenan's eyes flashed in anger. He waved his hand, and myriad paths—like unpaved roads—formed like patterns stretching across the desert. "So go. You're far stronger than you admit. You might not be able to live in a city, but you can leave *here*."

"There's nowhere else I want to be. After the years of ice,

I like the warmth, and"—she glanced at the distant cliff again—"what I've found here."

Keenan made a noise of irritation, but he kept his silence, and she felt no need to explain herself further, not to him. She could leave if she thought there was somewhere she'd be freer, happier, but it had only been here in the desert where she'd come close to happiness. When she'd first been freed from the cold, she'd wandered, but there was no peace in it. Since she'd made that ill-fated choice to attempt to be the queen Keenan sought, she'd been unhappy. It was only recently that she'd come near to the sort of happiness she'd always wanted.

Because of Jayce.

There was no way she'd tell Keenan about him; faeries had a long-standing tradition of cruelty to humans, and now that Keenan had no need to seek among them for his missing queen, she wasn't entirely sure what he'd do. There were whispers of rumors, murmurs that he was even fonder of mortals lately, but he also had a peculiar possessiveness toward all of the faeries who he'd chosen in hopes that they would be his queen. He might have rejected her, but that didn't stop him from acting like she would always belong to him.

"What do you want?" she asked.

"I wanted to tell you that I'm unbound and that Donia's . . . the new Winter Queen." Keenan's eyes clouded at the mention of the Winter Girl who'd replaced Rika, the one who'd become Winter Queen when he'd found his

Summer Queen. Overhead, clouds formed, their darkness matching his expression as a summer storm rumbled over the desert. In mere moments, the shadows of the clouds on the ground stretched and darkened. He was still tempestuous, perhaps more so than when she'd first met him, only now he had the strength to go with his moods.

"I know. All the desert fey heard. Donia will be a good queen." Rika smiled at the thought of Donia's ascendency. She, too, was originally mortal, and she'd made the same foolish mistake that so many girls had—to love Keenan and risk everything. Rika grinned before adding, "She'll be good at standing against you too, especially since she hasn't forgiven you."

Lightning hit the ground behind her, and Rika laughed at him. Like so many of those born faery, he was a petulant child sometimes. When she'd first become fey, such outbursts frightened her. Now, she knew that he was merely stomping his foot in a way that only he could.

"And you have?" He stood, and both of the chairs crumbled.

Rika didn't bother moving, letting herself lean into the collapsing chair, watching the streams of sand flow over her leg into the rips in her jeans. She grinned up at him from the desert floor. "No, but my forgiveness doesn't matter as much, does it?"

Keenan's face was emotionless, but lightning jags around them revealed the emotion that his face didn't. Despite the bright display of his volatile temper, he still spoke as if he were calm: "If you need anything, I am there to call upon."

"Actually Sionnach is *here* if I need anything." She held Keenan's gaze. "I'm solitary. Those of us in the desert . . . we don't belong to you even now that you're stronger. That won't change."

"If you need me—"

"There would be a price, and I've more than paid my dues for your 'help.' I learn from my mistakes."

The rain hit, soaking her, but sizzling to steam before it touched him. "The Summer Court is stronger," he said. "But because of the changes, things will be unstable for now . . . even out here. Not everyone's happy with the power shift."

Although Rika was wet and sand-covered, she felt victorious as she sat on the desert floor and mocked the Summer King's understatement. "You think? We already know that."

She looked up at him, wishing he was most anywhere but here, wishing he wasn't still so beautiful, wishing she didn't understand how the curse had hurt him too. She didn't truly hate him, but she didn't want to feel sorry for him. Softening toward him was dangerous. That truth was unchanging. "What do you *really* want, Keenan?"

"I want to protect you, to take you under my court's protection."

She shook her head. "I don't need you."

"I—"

"I *don't*," she repeated. "I can't lie because of what you made me. So let me say it again: I don't need you, and I don't want you in my life in *any* way."

The Summer King was nothing if not persistent though. He'd fought for nine centuries to reach the strength he had only just found. His sunlit skin glowed as he told her, "I can't lie either, Rika: I do want to protect you. Make a vow of fealty to me, and I will keep you safe if the coming troubles reach the desert."

"A vow? To *you*? No." She stood and brushed the sand from her jeans. "Are we done here?"

"Other solitaries have joined my court. . . . It's not so odd." In that instant, Keenan looked so earnest—genuine and eager, so like the boy she'd loved. It hurt more seeing him looking at her so familiarly, but then she reminded herself that he had always sounded exactly like that when he'd successfully manipulated her. This time, he wouldn't succeed.

"You could talk to the others out here," he added. "The solitary fey will listen to you, and—"

"No," she interrupted, foolishly hurt that he still saw her as a means to an end, a piece in a puzzle to be moved at his will. "I won't ask them to join the Summer Court."

As Keenan stepped closer to her, Rika had to grit her teeth to keep from backing away. Winds spun around them, as if it were just the two of them together, apart from the world, as she'd once believed it would be. He didn't reach out to touch her as he would've when she was human, but in the same tone that had haunted far too many of her dreams over the years, he whispered, "I never meant to hurt you.

You *know* me, Rika. It's a simple vow. Then my court can step in if anyone needs—"

"Your court isn't needed in *my* desert, Keenan. We handle things differently out here, and we have no business in court matters. The courts are a world away."

"You're being foolish, Rika. Letting grudges get in the way of what makes sense. Just talk to them."

He obviously wanted a way in to the loyalty of the desert fey, and so he was here now whispering regrets and tender words, but she wasn't a naïve girl, not now, not for decades. She turned and walked away from him, and she didn't look back even though she could feel the swirls of sand stirring as he resisted his anger.

After a moment, a gust of wind lashed against her back, and she knew he'd left.

Melodramatic as always.

Chapter 2

Thinking about the past was something Rika steadfastly tried to avoid, but seeing Keenan dredged up old memories. She shivered, and even the desert heat suddenly wasn't warm enough to counter the remembered chill. She shook her head as tears slid down her cheeks. Angrily, she wiped them away and looked toward the mortals in the distance climbing up the rock wall of one of the canyons. Three motorcycles—two with saddlebags and camping gear strapped down—were parked in the shadow of the canyon.

"At least *they* can't see me." Rika wanted to run toward them, to be near the mortals, to be far from where she'd spoken to the faery king, but she kept her pace, slowing briefly only as she passed some jumping cholla cactus. It didn't truly jump, but like the sweetly named teddy-bear cholla, the spines were easily detached. She'd learned that lesson in her earliest days in the desert. Like some of the native desert fey, some of the plants here were beautiful but would cut her skin with only the barest touch. It was one of the things she liked about the Mojave: here, the faeries weren't hiding their true nature behind court manners and pretty words. She liked the extreme honesty of the desert and many of its inhabitants.

As Rika walked across the sand, a soft smile crept over her face as she saw one of those inhabitants, the first mortal to draw her attention so intensely since she'd become fey. Jayce was, like the world around him, *real*. She wanted to speak to him even more than usual, to lose herself in a conversation with him. She couldn't. If he wasn't interested in her, it would crush her.

"It would probably be a mistake," she lectured herself, but she still stared at Jayce. Even the lingering clouds that reminded her of Keenan's visit weren't enough to completely convince her that her interest in Jayce was wrong.

The faeries in the desert didn't come near her as she passed them. They never did, but they stood so that she couldn't help but see them watching her. Like most desert dwellers, they peered from where they were half-hidden behind the shelter of canyon walls, eyelet canyons, and caves. The faeries who were out in the direct sun moved with a languid gait that said time was somehow more than infinite here.

Although they didn't approach, they did call out at her from various directions, making it clear that she was surrounded. Although the desert might look empty to those unfamiliar with it, there was always life—both natural and supernatural—all around her.

"Rika. Hey Rika."

"Come 'ere."

"No, over here."

Numerous faeries smiled and beckoned her nearer. Some smiles seemed friendly; others appeared menacing. Rika looked around, tracking where they all were, assessing whom she'd fight first if necessary.

Too many for me to handle if they attack me.

She didn't expect an attack, but they undoubtedly knew that Keenan had visited her. They'd be tense as a result. The desert faeries didn't belong to the faery courts; they existed in a hierarchical system of strength and dominance, not under the control of monarchs. Like all solitary faeries, the desert fey had an Alpha or co-Alphas, faeries who were the strongest and kept order of a sort. If a faery didn't like it, she could simply leave—or challenge the Alpha for dominance. If Rika challenged the Alpha, she'd win, but she'd never wanted power—even when she'd risked everything at the chance of being Keenan's missing queen. All she'd ever wanted was to be loved as she'd first thought Keenan had loved her.

"Where's Sionnach?" Rika called to the watching faeries. *He* was their current Alpha, had been so as long as Rika had lived in the desert. He was also the closest thing she had to a real friend. He'd long ago decreed that she was not to be overly harassed. For solitaries, that was as good as it got.

"He's out playing," said Maili, a faery girl with sand-striated skin and short spiky hair. Her face was expressionless, and her eyes were solid black. She fluttered her two-inch-long nails, making her already elongated fingers look even more stretched.

Another faery, mostly hidden in shadows, said, "Sionnach is out wooing mortals again."

"Which means he's not anywhere near here." Maili grinned. Aside from Sionnach and Rika, she was the strongest of the desert fey. If not for Rika's decision to stay out of the politics and power squabbles in the desert, they'd have been at each other's throats a decade ago. That didn't mean Maili didn't try to provoke conflict at every opportunity; it merely meant that they'd never come to serious blows.

As Rika watched, Maili waved at a group of faeries just a bit farther away—near the humans standing atop a small cliff. The faeries scrabbled up and across the rocks like misshapen crabs. They were almost human in their appearance, but with a worn meanness. Unlike Rika, they'd never been mortals, but always something *Other*. After so long in the desert, Rika didn't usually notice their Otherness, but her conversation with Keenan had unsettled her and reminded her of their differences. No matter how long she'd been this—and it had been far longer than she'd been a human—she'd always be an outsider to them. She had been mortal; she had been a part of the faery courts. She was the reason Keenan, a faery king, had just walked across their desert. No matter that he'd cost her more than he would ever be able to cost them, she was not one of them.

Rika wanted to argue, to tell them that she was a part of their world now, but she'd held herself apart for so long she wasn't even sure she *could* be a part of the solitaries.

A word rang out, loud in the still of the desert. "Oopsy."

Suddenly, Jayce was pushed off the rocky ledge where he'd stood. He shifted with surprisingly quick reflexes for a mortal, angling himself to take the impact with his hip and side.

Rika didn't think, *couldn't* think; she simply reacted. In a breath, she was a blur across the remaining distance. The world felt like it sped and slowed all at the same time. The mortal—the *person*—who had finally made her feel like life was worth more than enduring, like living again could be possible, was falling.

And then she was under Jayce, catching him, and becoming visible in the process. She knew she looked far too frail to catch a mortal in her arms, so after a brief hesitation, she let her legs give out from under her and collapsed to the sand with a mortal atop her.

With Jayce *touching me.*

Limbs tangled, they were still on the desert floor. Neither spoke or moved for an awkward moment. Rika tried to soak in every feeling, to notice as much as she could since he was finally touching her.

Then he rolled to the side so he wasn't. "I'm so sorry. Did I . . . Are you . . ." He looked from her to the cliff and back at her. "Don't move. I'll get help and—"

"I'm fine." Rika scuttled backward. A rush of panic

washed over her. Despite the usual comfort she found in the vast openness of the desert, she felt suddenly cornered and stood, poised to flee. As calmly as she could, she repeated, "I'm fine."

Even in her panic, her gaze slid over him. Jayce's sleeve was torn, and his jeans were sand-caked. He had scratches on his face, and she knew that he must be in pain from the impact. Yet, despite his injuries, he was completely fixated on her. "You're in shock or something," he said. "Just sit down and—"

"You're bleeding." She pointed to the blood seeping through the sleeve of his badly ripped shirt. His clothes were often tattered and worn, and he'd been injured from climbs and skateboarding, but she'd never seen him bleed so much. She didn't like how it made her stomach feel.

One of the other mortals, Jayce's friend Del, came into view atop the cliff. Like Jayce, he looked pretty grungy, unlike his skater girlfriend, Kayley, who now joined him. Rika had watched them enough to know that Kayley might look like she didn't belong with a boy whose electric-blue hair stuck out from the edges of his bandana, but she was every bit the adrenaline seeker he was, often more so.

Del called down, "Kayley wants to know if you're broken."

Only Rika could see the faeries who circled Del and Kayley in a mockery of a dance.

"Want to see if you can catch two at the same time?" one faery asked. He ran a hand through Kayley's hair, lifting it and letting it fall into her face.

Absently, Kayley shoved her hair out of her face and stepped to the side.

The faery smirked.

Kayley might not know the cause, but she felt something. Mortals often reacted without knowing what they were evading, chalking it up to wind or insects. Faeries took amusement in it. Such was the normal order of things.

This time, however, Rika tensed. These mortals mattered. Even though they'd never spoken to her, they were the closest things she had to friends in the human world. The faeries who circled them knew it; they knew exactly how to hurt her—and right now, they wanted to hurt her.

All because Keenan had visited.

"Jayce?" Kayley prompted, sounding a bit more concerned now.

Oblivious to Del and Kayley's danger, Jayce stretched, bending both arms, shifting weight from foot to foot, testing his body before answering Del. "Just bruised and bloodied . . ."

Del stepped forward and tossed a rucksack down. "Steriwipes and bandages in here. Use 'em. We'll be down soon."

Then the two mortals walked away, breaking through the ring of faeries that they couldn't see, going farther back on the cliff where they were out of sight.

While they were talking—and Jayce wasn't looking at her—Rika had started walking away. She wasn't up to dealing with the confrontational faeries or the fact that she'd revealed herself to mortals. She couldn't become invisible just yet in case one of the mortals looked her way and caught her, but she might be able to quietly slip away.

When Jayce turned, he called "Hey!" and came after her. As he reached her side again, he added, "Hold up."

"I need to be gone." She stepped farther away.

Jayce held his hands up. "I didn't mean to hurt you. It was an accident. . . ." He glanced briefly at the cliff. Del and Kayley were well away from the edge, and since he couldn't see the faeries on the edge of the cliff, he saw nothing amiss.

Rika, however, could see the faeries watching; several were now sitting in postures akin to gargoyles. They perched and watched her. She knew that their irritation was a result of Keenan's meddling in the desert, but she had no idea what to do about it. Later, she'd talk to Sionnach, but for now, all she could do was get away from the mortals, draw the surly faeries' attention away from them.

Jayce frowned. "It felt like a gust or . . . maybe the edge gave . . ." He shook his head and proceeded to do what mortals typically did when confronted with the impossible: he created plausible explanations. Then, he added, "It doesn't matter."

One of the faeries waved at Rika, and she tensed. Jayce's back was to them; all of his attention was fixed on her. There had been days during which she was invisibly at his side and wanted this very thing, but now that he was looking so intently at her, she wanted to flee. Behind him, the faeries watched too attentively, not actively threatening her or the humans but observing everything so carefully. It had been selfish of her to let on that she cared for the mortals; she saw that now.

And it was selfish of Keenan to come here.

It didn't matter though. Solitary faeries could not strike a king, but they could strike her or the humans. As calmly as she was able, she told Jayce, "I'm not angry; I'm not hurt. I just need to go."

"Let me give you a ride. We can get you checked out. . . . I *fell* on you." Jayce was trying to comfort her, even though he was the one bleeding and injured. Much like he cared for meandering tortoises or wounded birds, he tried to nurture her too. "Please wait?" he asked.

The gentle tone in his voice made it impossible to resist. He was injured because of her attention, and even though she feared that her presence there beside him would make it worse, she couldn't refuse the plea in his voice. She took a step toward him, but almost faltered when he smiled at her. Seeing that smile actually directed at her was more heart-stopping than she could've imagined.

Quickly, she forced her gaze downward, but then blanched at the sight of his injury. He was ignoring it because he was more concerned with her well-being, but she couldn't tell him that she was completely uninjured, that it would take far more than catching a falling boy to hurt her. Instead she said, "I'll wait if you bind that. Sit down."

"What's your name?" He was still standing, as if he was

unsure whether she'd dart away or not. "I'm Jayce."

"Rika," she said as she walked over to collect the rucksack that Del had tossed down.

Several of the fairies on the cliff scrabbled down; others stayed at the edge, kicking their feet in the air. Maili had apparently joined them on the cliff while Rika's attention was on Jayce.

"What do you think he'd do if he saw us?" Maili taunted. "What if he knew what *you* were?"

A few of the faeries pelted Rika with rocks, mostly small, but a few larger stones were tossed at her.

Rika didn't back away from them despite the sudden rock shower. The rocks hurt, but not enough that it made her react. After years of carrying snow and ice inside a body not created for such things, it took far more than rocks to cause her to wince.

Jayce, however, couldn't see the faeries. All he saw were rocks falling. He called out from the ground where he was now kneeling, "Be careful."

"I'm fine." She scowled pointedly up at Maili. "It's a little *unstable* up there. Maybe it needs to be knocked down."

"Do you really think you can 'knock down' all of us, Rika?" Maili's smile grew wide with glee, no doubt thrilled to finally get Rika's temper stirred. "I'd love for you to try. . . ."

Undaunted, Rika smiled at her just as she'd smiled at Keenan earlier; today, she wouldn't object to a challenge.

Maili stilled, unaccustomed to seeing Rika ready to

fight, but she didn't move toward Rika. As she had so many times, the solitary faery postured and antagonized, but she never actually started the competition she seemed to want.

Rika mouthed, "You'd lose."

"C'mon, Rika. What's say we have at it? Just us . . . and you," Maili said.

If she were truly strong enough to challenge Rika, she wouldn't need to surround herself with faeries who toadied for her approval. A true contender for Alpha should be able to act as an individual, should be strong enough to be truly solitary. Maili only played at being a legitimate challenger.

"Rika? Do you see something up there?" Jayce asked from behind her.

Rika held Maili's gaze and said levelly, "Nothing important."

Then she turned her back to Maili and the rest of the faeries.

"You're making a mistake," Maili called. Rocks and a fine cloud of sand showered down around Rika.

Rika ignored the faery and the debris, looking instead at Jayce, who had taken off his bloodied shirt, baring a well-defined chest and sculpted abs. The shirt he'd had on was balled up in his lap, and she forced herself to look at the bloody clothing instead of at his bare skin. She had to remind herself that he'd already bled because she was interested in him. She'd caused that. No good came of faeries wooing mortals. When she'd been mortal, a faery's attention had cost her everything. Now, she'd already cost Jayce pain.

She kept her expression blank as she calmly walked to Jayce's side and handed him the rucksack.

He looked at the sand in her hair and on her skin and shook his head. "You're a strange girl, Rika."

She sat down near him, but not too closely. It was silly to react so strongly to the bare skin he'd exposed. She'd lived among faeries for longer than he'd lived, but she was still shy. She'd never surrendered the mortal sensibility she'd had forever ago—or maybe it was simply that she *liked* him. He'd certainly stripped off his shirt where she could see him before, but every other time, she'd been invisible to him. It was harder to hide her appreciative glances when he could actually see her. If he did notice, though, he didn't remark on it.

"When cliffs start tumbling on you, you might want to move *away* from the falling sand and rocks," he said in a light tone.

He leaned over and brushed sand off of her shoulder and biceps. It wasn't in any way affectionate, but she tensed. She swallowed, watching his hand intently as it touched her skin. She wasn't sure she could recall the last time anyone had touched her so casually. Keenan's touches were never casual, nor were Sionnach's very rare moments of contact. There was always intent, meaning, so much that was hidden under what was meant to be casual but never truly was. Jayce, however, was only being kind.

When he withdrew his hand, she was trembling as if she were the human girl she appeared to be. Her voice came out very softly and tentatively when she said, "I . . . I wasn't in danger. It was just a few rocks."

He paused, almost imperceptibly, but she'd studied him often enough that she noticed. After a breath, he said, "Feeling invincible? A good scare will do that, won't it?"

Rika made an agreeing noise.

Jayce pulled a wipe out of the rucksack and wiped the blood and sand from his arm. "But rocks falling like that can mean a bigger one is coming down too."

She ignored the topic at hand. She wanted to talk to him, but the faery inability to lie was making her feel tongue-tied. The age-old tradition among faeries was to use omission and misdirection when avoiding truths, as Keenan had done, but she'd spoken so often to Jayce when he was unaware of her presence that she'd rather skip any topic altogether than misdirect.

"Do you need help?" she blurted.

"I'm good." He bound his arm, wrapping the bandage around it tightly. "I was up there for a while. You'd think I'd have seen you down here, but it was like you just appeared out of empty air. . . ." His words trailed off as he stared at her as if he was looking at her as *her*, not a girl he fell on. He smiled at her again like she'd dreamed he one day would.

The temptation was too much: she gave in and touched his arm, not a caress, but contact. "Don't stand so close to the edge next time, okay? Please."

He said nothing. Her hand was on his skin, and they were both motionless, staring at each other.

"But I wasn't too close—" He glanced at her hand, and then back at her. "I know this might sound crazy after I fell and just about crushed you, but do you want to do something later?"

She opened her mouth, but no words came out. The last time anyone had shown romantic interest in her was well over a century ago, when she was mortal, when she had no idea that faeries were real. She couldn't remember how to do this, how to be a girl next to a boy.

No good comes of faeries pursuing mortals, she reminded herself. *I can't do this.*

Panicked, she looked at the cliff. The faeries were gone.

"I need to go," Rika announced, and then she turned and ran, not as fast as she could, because that would be the sort of thing any mortal would notice as *Other*, but fast enough that there was no way Jayce could catch up to her.

Chapter 3

Hours passed as Rika sat inside the cave she'd called home for years. Only one lamp cast light in the shadows, and the fire pit remained cold. The desert heat was enough that she wasn't uncomfortable, but the chill had begun to creep into her home. Rather than do anything about it, Rika curled on her pallet in the shadows, hiding like an injured animal. Water ran through the side of the cavern in a little fissure, and the sound of it calmed her a bit.

"I can't risk it. Not again." She spoke the words to no one in particular. Like most of her conversations, there was no one to reply to her complaints. She'd chosen this life, the solitude she'd found here in the cave in the desert, far from the faery courts, separate even from the desert fey.

She'd tried. *Before. Before the winter, before I lost everything. . . .* That had been a mistake. *Love is a mistake.*

She forced herself to remember, to dredge up the thoughts that would help her stick to her resolve. She remembered sitting at a table with Keenan. He had looked human, too. She didn't know it then, but now she knew that he was hiding his true self under a glamour, an illusion faeries create to mislead mortals.

He holds her hand in his, staring at her intently. She blushes. He's wearing fine clothes, fashioned from cloth nicer than her best dresses. Even his most modest attire speaks of wealth greater than anyone she's met. Despite that, he doesn't look askance at her faded dress—or her plain home. She's never seen his home, but she's imagined how different it must be. Her home is filled with simple handcrafted wooden furniture, and not much of it, but it is clean and orderly. She's softened the sparseness with the bouquets of flowers he's brought.

"Come with me? Please?" he pleads, and she can't think of how she could deny him anything. Keenan's very presence brightens everything, and he wants her to be his, to love him and stand by his side.

Rika answers the only way she can, "Yes."

He pulls her to her feet and embraces her, as he whispers, "You are the one I've been waiting for. You have *to be her. . . ."*

In her cave, Rika wiped away tears as she remembered the hope she felt that day, the warmth that permeated her entire being. She'd believed that he loved her as she had loved him, that she had found a man who would cherish and protect her.

She had been so very wrong.

* * *

The ground is covered with snow, but as Keenan walks toward her his skin glows as if flames flicker just under the surface, the ground at his feet roils as it melts and churns. She knows now that he is not human, that he is something exceptional, *a king. She feels like she's in the middle of a fairy tale, on the verge of her very own happily ever after.*

He is barefoot, a golden effigy too beautiful to look at or to look away from. "You understand that if you are not the one, you'll carry the Winter Queen's chill until the next mortal risks this?"

She nods. This isn't the wedding ceremony she'd expected. It's better though. The boy she's fallen in love with is a faery, a magical being who has chosen her *to love. She's about to become fey too, because he picked her to be his queen. There's a risk; she knows that, but they are in love, and love will break the magic spell binding him.*

"If she refuses me, you will tell the next girl and the next"—he moves closer—"and not until one accepts, will you be free of the cold."

"I do understand." She walks over to the hawthorn bush. The leaves brush against her arms as she bends down and reaches under it.

She sees the Winter Queen's staff. It is a plain thing, worn as if countless hands have clenched the wood, and she almost hesitates.

Then, behind her, he moves closer. The rustling of trees grows loud, and the brightness from his skin intensifies. He needs *her to do this.*

Her fingers wrap around the Winter Queen's staff.

His sunlight warms her, and his radiance makes her shadow fall on the ground in front of her. The heat grows as he whispers, "Please. Let her be the one. . . . Please. This time . . ."

She holds on to the wooden staff as she straightens. She turns to face him, blinking against the brightness that fills him. Until this moment, she has believed, but as she holds it, his light fades away and an impossible chill consumes her body.

Her skin covers with frost, and she collapses. Ice spreads out from under her now prone body, freezing the ground that had only moments before been boiling mud. She can barely move from the pain, and her teeth chatter as she tries to speak.

A very large white wolf approaches her, and she knows that the wolf is as magical as the boy she's fallen in love with. She rests her face in the wolf's warm fur, and then she turns her head to Keenan and says, "I'm sorry I'm not . . . her."

But he is walking away, no longer glowing, no longer even looking at her.

As she let the memories wash over her, Rika felt the tears that were slipping down her cheeks, and she wished that she had lit the fire before allowing herself to dwell on the folly of love. More years than she ever expected to live had passed since those days, but the chill was hard to forget, even here.

"Always a princess, never a queen."

She looked up at the words, even though she knew who had spoken. No one else had the audacity to enter her home without her consent.

"Sionnach," she greeted him quietly.

The fox faery leaned against the wall at the mouth of the cave. He smiled at her, flashing her the sly smile that he wore more often than he wore a shirt. Even though he had the only true authority in this desert, he was poised on her threshold like he hadn't a care in the world. Unlike some of the other desert fey, Sionnach looked more human than Other, but he still had telltale foxlike features. His short auburn hair wasn't remarkable, but his eyes were—angular and large, those eyes could drown a person. His cheeks were edged too sharply, and his movements were quick and agile, emphasizing the fact that even with his almost-human appearance his actions often seemed alien. The way he stood hid his fox tail from her view, and in the shadows, his pointed ears were barely noticeable. In all, though, most of his features were just enough out of normal mortal proportions that a person wanted to look longer, but not so Other that they were unsettling. The glamour he donned around humans was primarily to hide his tail and ears.

"I hear that pretty boy visited you, *and* that you were playing with the mortals. . . ." He came closer as he spoke, but he didn't walk directly toward her. He slid farther into the cavern. Years ago, his peculiar way of moving when he was inside struck her as unsettling, but now she knew that it was simply how Sionnach was: he walked almost sideways into the cave in a skittish way that revealed that he was not comfortable inside, even if that *inside* was only a cave. He was shy, long ago earning himself the nickname of "Shy" as a result.

"I loathe this den of yours," he complained as he leaned

on a thick stalagmite almost beside her, one foot crossed over the ankle in a pretense of ease. This, too, was his way, posturing as if he were among the court fey. If Rika had not lived among the courts, Sionnach's carefully casual mien might intimidate her as it did the others in the desert.

"If you hate it, don't visit." Rika glared at him, embarrassed that he'd seen her tears even though he didn't remark on her wet cheeks.

A coy smile came over him. "No chance of that. You'd be even more miserable without me."

When she didn't answer, he dropped down beside her, cross-legged, and rested his elbows on his knees. He folded his hands under his chin and stared at her. "What with all of these new habits, are you going to go out roaming with me next? Venture out visibly? . . . Or are you going back with the pretty boy now that he's not so impotent?"

"No. No. And NO." She sighed and looked away. Tears blurred her vision again, and she wished that she could pretend to be unmoved by Keenan's visit and her subsequent encounter with Jayce. She'd spoken to Keenan often enough over the years to be beyond her emotions, but knowing that he'd finally found his missing queen had stirred up old hurt. There truly *had* been a mortal who wouldn't suffer for having been chosen by him. Rika simply hadn't been her.

Without knowing the specifics of what she'd been worrying over, Sionnach knew Rika well enough that he caught her face in his hands and made her look at him. "Temper suits you better than self-defeat, princess."

She couldn't speak. It wasn't often that Sionnach was serious. Often, he'd cajole or tease when she was sad, but rarely did the fox resort to seriousness. She'd heard the shift in his tone just now. He continued, "The Summer King doesn't deserve your tears. He never did."

"I know," she said, but she was still crying.

One hand cupped her face. With the other, Sionnach caught a tear on his fingertip as it slid down her cheek and then licked it from his finger. "Not ice. Not now. Not ever again."

But I'm still cold, she thought.

She couldn't say those words, couldn't admit that she could feel the chill too strongly when her memories washed over her, so she said, "I hate it when he comes here."

"Me too." Sionnach lowered his hand from her face and scooted back just a little. He teased, but she'd never taken his teasing or his assurances as something more. Tonight was no different. The fox's seriousness faded, and his smile grew dangerous. "But, it'd be silly of you to be here pouting while irritable faeries break that mortal you keep watching. . . ."

"What?" she gasped.

Sionnach shrugged, but his eyes twinkled with trouble. "They're mad at pretty boy, mad at you, so they're in a mood. You know how they get."

"But—"

"You saved the mortal," Sionnach reminded her. "You can't be surprised that they felt petulant about it."

"Why didn't you stop—"

"Your mortal shouldn't be my concern." He widened his already enormous eyes in a beguiling look. "You should have enough time . . . *if* you go now. He's at the railroad tracks."

"You're such a pain." She shoved him backward, any flash of tenderness she felt for him thoroughly quashed.

In that faery-quick way, Sionnach rushed to the mouth of her cave alongside her. Then he stopped, going no farther, but as she raced past him, he murmured, "You needed a distraction, princess."

CHAPTER 4

Inside the town of Silver Ridge, everything was faded. In the desert around the town, the colors were the beautiful hues of cactus and desert wildflowers, vibrant skies and impossibly rendered clouds, shimmers of serpents and flutters of birds. Silver Ridge, however, had a weathered tone. Sand and heat consumed everything here, but even so, the town had a beauty all its own. The buildings were a strange mix, as if architecture from various times and places had been thrown together in a weird hodgepodge.

Rika remembered when Silver Ridge was only a speck of a possibility, when adventurous miners came here in search of fortunes, when their families put down roots, and when the mishmash of people became a town. The peculiarity of knowing the town's history so well comforted her as she walked. She'd watched this small outpost of humanity grow in the great expanse of nature; she'd walked among them and drawn portraits of their faces as they came, aged, and died. She felt protective of the mortals who lived there now, but several in particular evoked a fiercer sense of concern.

She stopped midway into town, not wanting to get too close to the railroad tracks that stretched like a line of beautiful poison on the earth. Steel, because it was created from iron, was poisonous to faery. Humans—without knowing why they gravitated toward the steel—often lingered here at the edge of the tracks. A few decades ago, they'd created a park of sorts, filled with metal sculptures and benches, but even before that, mortals had clustered here since the tracks had been installed.

On the edge of the rail yard were faeries who had been stopped by the metal as if it were a wall they could not climb. They watched the mortals: Jayce, Del, and Kayley. Del no longer wore his bandana, and Rika noticed that his blue mohawk now had white tips. It suited him, his vibrant hair against his suntanned skin, but it struck her as being so different from Jayce. Del's mohawk with its ever-changing color was much like his carefully chosen clothes: proof that he put time into looking like he didn't worry over his appearance. By contrast, Jayce truly didn't pay much attention to the way he looked. He had a splash of color in his dark dreads, but that had been a whim. Rika knew; she'd watched. Everything about Jayce was as real with or without an audience; she admired that about him.

Rika passed the faeries, putting herself between them and the mortals. She could go closer to the dangerous metal than the other faeries could because she'd been mortal first, but she still couldn't walk all the way up to it. Being even this close to the steel made her queasy and weak. Fortunately, the nearby faeries couldn't approach it either, but sooner or later, Jayce would have to leave the protection of the railroad tracks and thus become vulnerable.

Although she wasn't convinced that they would actually harm him, she couldn't risk it. She made a noise, not quite a word but the start of one, before she realized what she'd done. Much like seeing him fall and reacting without thought, she'd done the same thing now. The result was the same as well: she'd begun talking to Jayce when he could see her. By her choice, she'd broken her own rules on keeping him at a safe distance.

Before she could think of how foolish it was, Jayce turned his head and saw her. "It's you. . . ." He smiled and took a hesitant step toward her. "Where did you come from?"

Rika didn't move. She opened her mouth to speak, to find some answer that was true. She settled on, "Out there."

She made a vague gesture northeast, toward the desert, or more accurately, much farther away, across an ocean to a land where it grew cold, where there were seasons and so much greenery that her heart ached a little to think of it. *Home.* She couldn't stand being there now, not after so long with winter's pall on her, but she still remembered the beauty.

Jayce left Del and Kayley, moving farther from the safety of the railroad tracks. "You look like you're not feeling well."

When she didn't answer, his arm went around her. He led her toward a wooden bench. *Farther still from the tracks.* Palm trees, looking battered and still proud despite it, cast narrow shadows.

"I knew we should've had you checked out. I couldn't figure out how you vanished, where you were hiding. I looked in the caves where we were. I—" He stopped himself nervously before continuing, "I almost thought you were a dream, but Del saw you too."

She stared at Jayce. Bruises shadowed his cheek. His ripped shirt had been replaced, but this one looked tattered too. A steel chain-link bracelet hung on his left wrist. Fortunately, since he held her with his right arm, the steel wasn't likely to brush against her and injure her.

"Are you real, Rika?" he asked quietly.

"I'm real," she assured him. That part she could say with certainty.

"Are you sure? You seemed almost like a dream earlier, vanishing when I looked away." He was flirting, but there was an undercurrent of something else there. He might not consciously know that she wasn't human, but an instinctive wariness in him tangled with a desperate hopefulness she'd seen when he drew his more fanciful images. Jayce caught her gaze as he said, "A beautiful girl shows up, saves me, and vanishes into the desert. . . . It's either a dream or magic."

Rika couldn't speak. *He thinks I'm beautiful.* She should be thinking about the fact that he was implying that she'd vanished, but it was his compliment that made her stare back at him in wonder.

"You did save me, you know. I'm not broken anywhere. Just bruises," he said in a voice so low that it felt like it was only the two of them in the world.

They were not alone though: not only were there faeries, but Del and Kayley also stood nearby. Del was watching them. Rika could see the couple in her peripheral vision. Kayley spoke to him, but his attention was fixed on Jayce. Despite the twinge she felt at their protective gazes, she was grateful that Jayce had such good friends.

Jayce turned to look over his shoulder, noticing that Rika was looking past him. "They're okay." He looked back at her and smiled. "Are you always this shy?"

Without having quite meant to, Rika nodded. She wasn't used to talking to people. Months would pass when her only conversations were with Sionnach or with Jayce—who until today didn't hear her because of faery glamour. When she had been the Winter Girl, she hadn't exactly been beset by social invitations either. She spoke to whichever mortal girl Keenan tried to seduce, to Keenan, and to his advisors and court members. None of them had been faeries she could call friends: they all wanted Keenan to succeed; her job was to thwart him. Those were the terms of the curse that had ensnared her when he'd picked her for the test. If she'd been his missing queen, she would've freed him, been beside him for eternity. If she had refused the test, she'd have been his subject—one of the flighty Summer Girls who frolicked and danced. When she took the test and failed, she'd been cursed to carry winter *and* sworn to attempt to convince the next girl to refuse him. Even though she'd risked everything for Keenan—and lost—she'd been cursed to have to work against him as he tried to find the missing Summer Queen. Her situation hadn't exactly made her popular.

She forced herself to look only at Jayce. After an awkward silent moment, several heartbeats too long, Rika blurted, "I've watched you climb before."

What a stupid thing to say!

Jayce smiled though. "I wish I'd seen you then . . . maybe you wouldn't have run away earlier."

Tentatively, she said, "I don't need to run right now."

Despite how awkwardly she'd handled everything, he still seemed interested. "So do you want to walk"—he gestured at the benches—"or sit? We're probably both too sore to walk *too* far."

Faeries clustered closer, surrounding the bench. They didn't speak, chortle, or react. They just pressed too near, their bodies brushing against hers and his, making Rika tense. She should tuck him into some safe steel-walled house. *But I want to talk to him.* She shouldn't do it, but still she said, "Stay. I want to just stay here with you."

"Later," Jayce called to Del and Kayley. Then he put a hand on the small of her back. "There's a quiet spot out this way."

At the feel of his hand against her—even though there was a shirt between her skin and his hand—she hesitated, and then, shakily, let him guide her to a bench. Lingering with him felt more dangerous than anything she'd done since becoming a faery. There had only ever been one other boy she'd trusted, and he'd stolen *everything* from her. The fear and the memories of that mistake rushed back so intensely that she felt paralyzed and stopped mid-step.

"You said you didn't need to run; remember?" Jayce said.

She nodded and took another tentative step.

Behind them, faeries whispered. A number of them vanished in different directions, and she was silently grateful that they weren't going to challenge her here. Maybe Sionnach was wrong about the threat; maybe the faeries had better things to do. She didn't know, and just then, she didn't care.

All that mattered was that she was with Jayce. They walked toward a bench, and she realized that he still had his hand on her back. He was touching her, and they were alone together.

Chapter 5

Sionnach amused himself by flitting in and out of visibility around one of the somewhat nearby towns: starting a quarrel between strangers, kissing a mortal girl and fleeing while her eyes were still closed. *I'd rather be keeping an eye on Rika.* She was his priority, a project of sorts, but not every detail of his plan was something he could handle himself. It hadn't been easy, but he'd lured the skittish faery out of her cave. The next step was up to her; he just hoped she didn't screw it up. *Or find out what I'm doing.*

Dealing with Rika was one of the difficulties of being Alpha . . . or maybe it was a difficulty of being a fox faery . . . or maybe of trying to balance his personal goals and his duties to the desert fey. Sionnach wasn't sure what the *cause* of the challenge was, but it didn't really matter. The course was clear. Rika needed a nudge. She'd holed up in her cave licking her wounds for years—and he'd allowed it. He'd even supported it. Things had changed though. The

Summer King, a faery Sionnach loathed, had finally discovered his missing queen. For centuries, he'd wooed mortals looking for her. As a result of his affections, those mortal girls had all been cursed to become faeries. Two of those formerly mortal girls ruled faery courts now. The Winter Queen and Summer Queen were originally mortals. Worse yet, they were both mortals who'd cared enough for Keenan to risk everything. Word had already traveled to the desert about the growing hostilities between the two queens. The final pieces of a multi-court war were coming to bear: the High Queen had taken an interest in a mortal the Summer Queen loved, and the Dark King had bound himself to yet another mortal girl. As rulers, they'd all failed to think of the good of their courts, putting desire ahead of duty. It was precisely what Sionnach was trying to avoid. He *felt* desire aplenty, but he wasn't going to risk the safety of the desert fey for his own selfishness. He had to protect them. It was what being Alpha meant, and right now, he was risking everything he wanted in order to do just that. Trouble in the courts was growing, and only a fool would believe that conflict between regents wouldn't spill over to the rest of their world. Sionnach wasn't a fool . . . at least he hoped he wasn't.

"Sionnach?"

He turned and was relieved to see one of his fey spies.

The faery who'd come to deliver the report stood like a corpse, emaciated to the point that his eyes seemed vast in the narrowness of his face.

"Well?" Sionnach's whole body nearly twitched in

expectation. "Is she with him?"

"She is."

"And?" Sionnach felt the curl of excitement, of *possibilities*, in his stomach. He'd planned and schemed for years in preparation for this moment. Rika was like a hidden arsenal that he'd hoped not to use, but hope was different than reality. He'd still planned for the possibility. When he'd seen the way she watched the mortal boy, he knew the time was near. The mortal could be useful, and then *Rika* would be useful.

But then the Summer King had arrived, setting things into motion a bit sooner than Sionnach had planned, causing troubles as court faeries often did. Sionnach's tail twitched at the thought of the disruption. He'd adjusted, but it made for a more harried plan than he'd have liked. It was messier than it should be. Despite everything, he was finally near to seeing progress. Rika saw the lure and was tempted.

"And what happened?" he prompted his spy.

"She's with the mortal."

"Annnd?" Sionnach drew the word out while his hands flitted in the air as if he could gesture his way into bending reality to his will. Sadly, he couldn't.

The faery who'd carried the report to him was bright enough to know that there was an answer Sionnach sought *and* that he hadn't delivered that answer. Still he tried. "They sit on a bench, and they sort of speak to each other."

"Bo-ring. She's been watching him for months, and she's still—" Sionnach cut his own word off with a sigh.

He despaired of her sometimes. After all his patience, Rika continued to thwart his plans. He needed her to come out of hiding. He'd set the bait out, all but delivered the boy to her, and still she resisted.

Mortals passed by as he pondered what to do next. There *was* an answer, and he'd find it. He was as clever as the fox that he resembled, and perhaps also as unscrupulous. *Not quite.* If he were, he'd have been even *less* honest with Rika. As it was, he skirted the border of lies in encouraging her interest in the boy.

As he rolled the quandary around in his mind, a mortal caught his attention. She looked a bit like Rika: short hair and a tiny frame, fierce in her posture despite her diminutive size. Unlike Rika, the mortal girl was all wrapped up in jeans and a low-cut top designed to flaunt her body. Perhaps that was what he needed to clear his mind, a mortal who *looked* like Rika but wasn't likely to act like her. A flirtation would at least distract him. For all the talk of fey and mortals not mixing, there was something strangely appealing about time with mortals. Regent and solitary alike, faeries tended to be intrigued by mortals. Sionnach himself had dalliance after dalliance with them, none serious, all fleeting, but they fascinated him for long moments.

The girl paused as she noticed his attention. She smiled and then ducked her head.

Sionnach waited, watching as her gaze lifted to see if he watched her. *Yes. She'll do nicely.* He didn't look away from the new mortal as he instructed his spy, "Go threaten the boy. I'll be along momentarily."

The faery who'd brought the message loped off across the street, and Sionnach went to meet his newest mortal fascination.

"Carissa," she said by way of greeting. "And you are?"

"Shy."

"Really?" She offered him a smile that transformed her face, making her look less like Rika, but still lovely. "You don't seem very shy."

He ducked his head, feigning bashfulness for a moment, and was rewarded by her laughter. "It's a pet name for that very reason," he admitted. "I'm woefully bold, I'm afraid."

Carissa stepped closer. "Prove it."

This was why he appreciated mortal girls. He'd confessed that same thing to so many girls, fey and mortal alike, and he never knew what to expect of the mortals. Faeries were more predictable. In the world at large, he had only to look at their court to know how they'd respond, and here in the desert, he was their Alpha, so they wouldn't refuse his interest—which was precisely why he didn't woo any of them. There was no challenge if there was no risk of rejection, a stance some faeries didn't seem to understand.

The mortal girl was staring at him boldly, so he pulled her near, lowered his lips to hers, closed his eyes, and kissed her until she was unsteady on her feet. When she pulled back several moments later, her arms were twined around his neck, and her breathy words of approval were whispers against his skin. She was happy, and he wouldn't tell her that he pictured someone else when he closed his eyes. He'd only slipped and admitted *that* once.

For a moment, he stood with his eyes still closed and enjoyed the illusion, but he didn't have the luxury of spending his evening standing in the shadows kissing a stranger. He had plans to tend. Reluctantly, he opened his eyes and looked at Carissa. She really was quite pretty in her own right.

"I have to go," he began.

She pulled a phone out of her jeans pocket. "Number?"

Sionnach shook his head and patted his empty pockets. "No phone."

"Really?"

"Truly."

Carissa looked at him like he'd just confessed to living a life lacking electricity, automobiles, and internet. He smiled. None of those were a part of his life, but they were easy to hide. The lack of a mobile phone stood out though.

She looked around the street. It was mostly empty. A few older mortals pushed a baby carriage nearby; a weathered man scowled at something he'd heard on his headphones. There were, however, some girls sipping their drinks and laughing. After a moment, she took his hand and tugged him toward them. Amused, he followed.

"Do any of you have a pen?" she said when they reached the girls.

Two of them stared at her silently, but a third girl searched in her purse. What she pulled out of the bag, though, was an eyeliner pencil. She held it out. "This is the best I've got."

Carrisa—who still hadn't released his hand—took it, used her thumb and finger to slide the cap off and into her palm, and then caught Sionnach's gaze. "Pull up your sleeve."

He obeyed.

"*This*"—she scrawled digits on his skin—"is my number." She blew on the skin as if the makeup needed to dry. Then she started to write again. "And my name. Call me."

Sionnach glanced at the numbers and back at her eyes. "I'll see you again," he promised. He wasn't sure about the calling her part, but he would see her. He leaned in and kissed her again, gently this time, and then walked away still smiling. He didn't think mortals and faeries had anything but ultimate sorrow in their lives if they tried to spend eternity together—mortals died far too quickly and easily for that—but he wasn't looking for forever. He already had plans for his forever.

As he stepped into the shadows, he faded from visibility again and began to run back to Silver Ridge. If he could get the final pieces in place, the day would be a victory. He'd hoped to be away from the town today, to stay out of the way so his feelings didn't sway him from his plans, but that hadn't worked. Now, he had to go meddle in Rika's life and hope he didn't lose sight of the goal.

Chapter 6

The area near the tracks in Silver Ridge wasn't somewhere Rika usually lingered, and she wasn't sure how long she could stay there. Now that they sat on a bench, the tracks weren't near enough to cause her pain, but being near Jayce like this hurt. She'd grown so accustomed to being near him without his knowledge that she struggled with trying to figure out how close she could be now that he could see her.

They sat on the bench, very carefully not touching—in sharp contrast to Del and Kayley, who were standing a short distance away, so caught up in each other that they were seemingly oblivious to the world around them. But Rika was careful to keep a distance between her and Jayce. She told herself that it was to protect him, as if not touching would somehow trick the desert fey who watched, as if they didn't already know that she was half in love with the mortal boy.

Although Rika could hear a group of faeries approaching

her, she didn't react. The town and the desert were filled with fey things. Many were harmless. She hoped that these were such faeries—until she saw them. They were some of the faeries who'd been on the edge of the cliff, and they were headed straight toward the bench where she sat with Jayce.

"She can't stop us."

"We ought to be allowed to play."

"Keenan probably told her to spy on us." Maili's voice stood out from the rest, and Rika knew that if Maili came near, she would force the confrontation she'd wanted earlier. She probably wouldn't don a glamour to appear human, so Rika would be left looking like she was swatting at empty air—or she'd have to endure an attack without reacting. Neither option sounded appealing.

Rika grabbed Jayce's hands. "Can we go inside?"

"Inside where?"

Her gaze darted around. The only place nearby was a multilevel, tile-roofed, yellow-walled building where clusters of mortals were coming in and out. She pointed. "There."

"Umm."

"Please?" She stood and tugged so that he came to his feet beside her.

The faeries were almost too near now. Although Jayce couldn't see them, he'd obviously noticed Rika's tense posture and expression. He turned away to call out to Del and Kayley. "Hey."

After a moment, his friends stopped kissing. Del, arms still around Kayley, answered, "What?"

"Dead Ends?"

Kayley shrugged and pulled farther away from Del. After they put their clothes to rights, Del and Kayley, each with an arm around the other, sauntered toward them. The couple was almost as bold as Summer Court faeries in their affection, and Rika couldn't help but think that there were traits that were as much mortal as fey.

Together Rika and the three mortals walked to the door of the club. Del and Kayley seemed like they were trying to be polite to her, but they weren't going out of their way to talk to her. Perhaps if she were someone else, their attitude would upset her, but considering how difficult she'd found even talking this slight amount, she was relieved by their feigned indifference. Plus, she'd watched them often enough to know that they weren't truly indifferent; until they determined if she was staying, they simply didn't see the need to bother getting to know her. They were Jayce's friends, and he didn't often date. He *did* have a lot of random conversations with girls he didn't ever spend a second night hanging out with. There was no reason for his friends to think they'd see a girl who showed up out of nowhere again the next day. *And they might not.* She'd *be* there, but that didn't mean they'd see her—they hadn't the past few months despite how often she'd been with them.

In comfortable silence, they joined the small cluster of people outside Dead Ends. Like the rest of the town, the people here reflected an odd mix of styles. Some people were dressed in what Rika considered elaborate costumes, while others wore clothes as casual as Jayce's were.

His hand tightened on hers as they joined the chaos inside Dead Ends—and she was grateful for his steady grip. The overflowing mass of people and thundering music made Rika want to flee.

Kayley and Del were being swept into a crowd of people, but Jayce didn't join them. He wound through the bodies, holding tightly to her. When they found a bit of space to themselves, he leaned in closer so she could hear. "Are you okay?"

"Crowds." She tried to smile, but she knew it must've looked pained because Jayce frowned and tried to lead her back outside.

"C'mon then," he said. "We'll leave."

But three of the faeries had followed them inside. Two were plainly visible to humans, looking as menacing as some of the humans were trying to appear. The third faery was Maili; she had stayed invisible to the swarm of mortals in the club.

"Let's go this way." Rika tugged Jayce deeper into the crowd, pushing through the room as she looked for another exit. Her attention flitted everywhere, on windows too high up to access, exposed pipes overhead, shadowed corners. There were no exits she could see, no way to get Jayce to safety.

She maneuvered him so he was in the thick of the crowd with her. It wasn't a complete solution, but she thought it would help.

Almost immediately, though, one of the faeries zipped toward them and clamped a hand down on Jayce's shoulder.

The faery tugged on Jayce, spinning him around and causing him to stumble. If not for the steel bracelet Jayce wore, he'd have been in a worse situation, but the bracelet brushed against the faery's exposed skin. The burn of it caused him to release Jayce.

Rika started to grab Jayce to pull him to safety.

The second faery grabbed Rika's hair. He was much bigger than her, so much so that his palm cupped the back of her skull like he was cradling a ball.

She glared and yanked back, tilting her head so her chin was pointing upward and her head was at an angle. "You really don't want to do this."

The faery tilted his head downward and tugged her so he was mouth-to-forehead with her. "Yeah. I do."

She darted a glance at Jayce. He was staring at the faery that had grabbed him.

"I'm still stronger than *any* of you out here," Rika whispered to the faery in front of her. Then, she headbutted him.

Surprised, he reached up to touch his face. Until now, Rika had avoided fighting with faeries. When they would act out, she always extricated herself. Tonight, though, she was tired of avoiding conflict. She kicked the faery, the heel of her foot slamming into his lower ribs, and he stumbled.

The mortals who were nearby started to back away.

Jayce glanced at her and, seeing that she was in a fight, looked worried. Almost in perfect synchronicity, they both took a swing at their attackers. The faery facing her winced at the impact, but the faery in front of Jayce laughed.

"What's your problem?" Jayce snarled at the faery, simultaneously trying to pull Rika behind him.

She was touched by the gesture, but mortals weren't strong enough to defeat faeries. She, however, was a faery fierce enough to defeat most anyone who stood against her. Such was the consequence of having been a Winter Girl. Choosing not to fight all of these years didn't mean she was unable; it merely meant that she'd been making a different choice. Tonight, she'd revised her plan.

The mortals around them watched the growing conflict. Rika stood beside Jayce, staring at the faeries who'd come here looking for trouble. "This is a bad idea," she told them.

The growing comprehension in their expressions said that they knew she was right, but they didn't retreat. Neither did she—or Jayce, for that matter. He had no idea of how capable she was. She looked tiny next to him, but it was her that the faeries were watching. Rika had avoided the desert quarrels and dominance disputes, so the faeries she faced weren't used to her fighting. They had no sense of her technique to rely on to help them. Even more, they were obviously shocked by her uncharacteristic behavior; they watched her warily, neither advancing nor retreating.

"Let's go." Rika started to back away, not looking away from them.

"Or not," Maili said as she joined them—finally visible to humans now. She held a knife that looked like a carved horn, sharp and primitive.

Rika didn't hesitate: she punched Maili, knocking her back hard enough that she landed on her backside on the club floor.

Maili's face twisted in an angry snarl.

Rika pointed at the knife. "*That* doesn't make you equal to fighting me."

For a moment, Jayce stood stunned beside her; then he grabbed her hand and pulled her with him deeper into the sea of bodies.

"What was *that*?" Jayce glanced over his shoulder at her as they moved away from the faeries.

Rika pretended not to hear him. There was no answer Rika could give without using lies or misdirection. All that mattered was getting Jayce away from danger. Later, she'd find a solution, but right now she needed to get him away from Maili. The faeries weren't going after the mortals in the club, but they were pursuing her.

Then—standing so near she almost ran into him—Sionnach was in front of her like a savior in a crisis. If she were the hugging sort, she would wrap her arms around him. Instead she tugged Jayce the rest of the way toward the fox faery.

"They're not making sense, Shy," she half yelled as she reached his side, and then promptly blushed as she realized that she called him by his pet name—*and* that she'd rushed to his side. "I mean, Sionnach . . ."

He grinned but didn't call her on either of her slips.

Beside her, Jayce grew suddenly still. He gave Sionnach a wary look, and then his gaze drifted from the fox faery to her. Rika hated that Jayce was involved in an altercation with faeries almost as much as she hated the suspicious looks he was giving her and Sionnach. She didn't want him to think that she'd misled him—and on her relationship to Sionnach, at least, she hadn't. What she was, what they'd fought, why he'd fallen earlier, those were all truths she couldn't share, but on the subject of her interest in him she had been true.

Jayce obviously had doubts, though. He released her hand.

"I'm sure they make sense, but *you* two being here doesn't. Come on." Sionnach looped an arm around her waist. Other faeries, those who were here with him, cleared a path through the crowd and then vanished when they reached a doorway.

Sionnach looked past her to catch Jayce's eye. "This way."

The fox faery held open the door so Jayce and Rika could step into a short hallway. It was starkly empty, except for a mortal girl who smiled widely at Sionnach as they approached. She'd been leaning against the wall with a dreamy expression on her face, looking at Sionnach like he was a god. Sionnach flashed her a blindingly sweet expression, but he didn't speak to her. Instead, he focused his attention on Rika, as if her slip into familiarity with him had changed something between them.

"What do you need?"

Rika stepped protectively close to Jayce. "I need to get him out of here."

Jayce started, "I can—"

"So go." Sionnach gestured to the door at the other end of the hall. "I'll stay and sort out the rabble. Take him to your den."

Rika hesitated. It made sense, but she couldn't begin to figure out how she'd explain *that* to Jayce. At the same time, she rebelled at the idea of abandoning Sionnach to face the faeries who'd started trouble. He wasn't flawless by any stretch of the imagination, but he was the closest thing she had to a friend in the desert, the only faery she almost trusted. "If they hurt you . . ."

Not surprisingly, Sionnach was amused at the idea. "You know better than that, princess. They're my responsibility anyhow. So go on; take your boy for a run."

Jayce raised both brows at Sionnach, but this time, he remained silent. The sound of an old horn interrupted the silence, and Jayce pulled out his phone. "Del texted," he said after a moment. "They split when things got weird in there. He doesn't like violence."

"Good," Rika said quietly, carefully not meeting Sionnach's gaze even as the fox faery stared at her.

"Take him home," Sionnach urged her again.

As he waited for her reply, his twinkling eyes and crooked grin were in such contrast to the chaos she could hear inside the club, as if he weren't at all disturbed by the way Maili had behaved, as if he weren't encouraging her to reveal secrets to a mortal. There were rules, actions faeries ought not engage in unless they wanted the courts coming round and starting to interfere.

"They can't do *that.*" Rika scowled in the direction of the main room, choosing to focus on the fight rather than the decision she needed to make. "They're out of hand. Starting trouble around . . . people. We can't ignore that."

"So I guess *we* need to figure out how to stop them. Leash them." Sionnach stared at her, waiting for her as he had so many other times over the years she'd known him.

Rika knew he was right, almost as much as she knew that getting involved with faery politics was exactly what she swore she wouldn't do. Sionnach had brought up her ability to be Alpha or co-Alpha often enough that she had threatened him with bodily harm the last time he'd mentioned it. After years of staying quietly away from the machinations and struggles of the solitary desert fey, she was about to be involved. In truth, she *was* involved now. She'd stood and fought against them, thereby ending years of uninvolvement. It was because of her interest in Jayce that this was all happening, and it was because of him that she would remain involved. She'd been the catalyst, and she couldn't expect Sionnach to handle it. He might help tonight, but tomorrow she had to begin to figure out what she should do. For now though, she told Sionnach, "Be safe. I owe you."

"I know." The fox faery glanced at Jayce again and then gave Rika a long, unreadable look before turning and walking away.

Silently, Rika and Jayce went to the door and stepped outside.

So many broken rules. What's one more?

If she were honest with herself, she'd admit that there were times she'd wished she could tell Jayce that she existed, that she was near him, that she was a faery. She'd never expected it to happen, but here they were. She took a steadying breath and said, "We're going to run. No matter what happens, just keep moving your feet. *Run*, okay?"

Jayce gave her a look like she'd lost it. "Maybe I should just go."

For a moment, she considered letting him walk away. She could follow him invisibly; things could return to the way they were before she'd exposed herself to save him. That wasn't what she wanted though, so she reached out and entwined her fingers with his.

He didn't react, and for a moment, she thought he'd pull away and leave.

"Please?"

"I need some answers, Rika." He shook his head, but he didn't pull his hand away. "That whole scene inside was weird."

"Come with me, and I'll give you some answers." She held his gaze and repeated, "Please?"

After a moment, he nodded.

She smiled and then she said again, "*Really*. Don't forget to move your feet."

And then she started to run, holding on to Jayce's hand; she didn't go as fast as she had when she'd disappeared earlier, but she traveled fast enough that each of her steps was the distance of many of his. Her movement propelled them forward. His running merely kept his body upright.

The world blurred around them for an impossibly brief time, and then they were at a cliff in the desert. In the far distance behind Jayce was the town; he hadn't turned to see how far they'd traveled yet, staring instead at the cliff in front of them.

The moon was three-quarters full, and the desert was shadowed and beautiful in the night. Several night-dwelling animals were out. A coyote slunk by in the periphery; farther out, a bobcat crouched on a ledge.

"Welcome to my home."

"Where?" Jayce looked around now in confusion, finally noticing how far they'd run in a few brief moments. "How did we . . ." His words died as he stared at her.

Ignoring that question, she pointed to a small inlet in the rock face over their heads. "Grab there. Come on. We need to get inside."

"I *really* have questions. . . ." Jayce started.

"I know." Rika scaled the cliff using the almost imperceptible steps. She was a few feet off the ground before she urged, "Come with me."

With a strange bemused smile, Jayce shook his head and then climbed past her. "You're full of all sorts of surprises, aren't you?"

"You have no idea," Rika whispered.

CHAPTER 7

Jayce stood at the mouth of her cave—where Sionnach had stood earlier—looking not at her but at the expanse of desert they'd crossed. "That isn't possible, you know. Moving that fast, that far."

Rika stepped in front of him, but instead of answering the question he wasn't quite asking yet, she told him, "We're safe here."

"Who were they? Why were—"

"I can't answer that," she said softly.

"She had a knife. That girl . . ." Jayce pulled his attention from the desert and glanced at Rika finally.

"I know." She kept her expression unreadable, hating that she already had to act so much like a faery instead of the girl she'd wished she could be with him, but she was what she was. "She'd use it too. If you see her, just get away."

"You're . . . what sort of fight school do you belong to? Someone as tiny as you—" He stopped mid-sentence and gave her an intense look. "You're a little scary, Rika."

She turned her face away. "I'm sorry. I shouldn't have . . . And we shouldn't . . . I didn't see any other way. You were in danger."

He put a hand on her cheek, tentatively. When she looked at him, he whispered, "I didn't say scary was a bad thing."

"Oh." She didn't move any closer to him, even though there were very few things she could imagine wanting more than being closer to him. *This is a mistake.* She was frozen, unable to either close the distance or retreat.

They stood there awkwardly for a moment.

And then he lowered his hand and stepped back a little. "So show me around your home?"

As they walked farther into the cave, Jayce didn't ask about the oddity of living here. Instead, he took her hand in his. In his other hand, he held a lantern she'd given him. Silently, they wandered through the labyrinth of tunnels. He trusted her to lead him, and she marveled silently at the gift of his trust.

Tentatively, she led him to an immense room. Pipe organ stalactites and cascading veils hung like precious art. Smaller passageways led from the room, and several more camping lanterns sat on the ground beside their feet. She lit one, bringing a bit more light to the immense cavern. Above them in the shadows, the faint shape of some of the colony of bats that nest in the caves stirred, but didn't flee. They had become used to her over time.

"I've never brought anyone in here. They're my company."

She gestured at the bats and then laughed self-consciously, realizing that she sounded nervous and more than a little peculiar.

Jayce didn't laugh. Instead, he whispered, "They're beautiful. The whole place is—" He stopped and looked intently at the far wall, at the mural she wanted to share with him. He lifted his lantern higher as he walked toward it. "Amazing."

Rika couldn't move. She stayed frozen in the center of the cavern, feeling extra vulnerable and trapped despite the vast cavern. She'd seen *his* art so often, but she hadn't shared her art with more than a handful of people in her life.

Jayce was wide-eyed as he studied her art. "This is incredible. It's not *old* though. I've seen cave art. This is new. . . . But the materials . . ." He walked along the wall, gaze fixed on the art, occasionally glancing at the uneven ground at his feet as he walked. Although the mural extended as far as the light reached and beyond, he stopped after a few moments and looked back at her. "Did you do this?"

She shrugged. "I get lonely. I needed to talk, and there was no one . . . so I did that."

"Art to talk . . . Yeah. I get that." Jayce nodded, watching her as he said it. It was the same look of wonder he'd had when he'd first seen her, before the weirdness, before the fight, before their run across the desert. "It's hard to find words sometimes."

"Or anyone trustworthy enough to listen." She walked over to stand beside him.

"I draw. Not like *this*, but . . ."

Suddenly, the bats stirred en masse as they heard a voice calling into the tunnels, "Princess? Come out; come out."

The whole colony seemed to leave in one black wave, and for a moment, Rika and Jayce stood together silently watching the bats.

"That's Sionnach, from earlier. He's here," Rika babbled awkwardly.

Jayce's expression clouded at the intrusion, but he was silent as she took his hand in hers. His fingers were warm, and for a moment, she wanted to stay silent and hidden with this boy who understood the need to speak with art. That wasn't an option though; she'd indebted herself to the fox faery who was waiting for them.

"Come on," she said.

They followed the twisting maze of tunnels to the first cavern they'd entered when they came into the cave. Sionnach's back was to them, and Rika could already see that there were various scrapes visible on his arms, as if something with talons slashed him. When he turned to face Jayce and Rika, more injuries became visible.

"I need to talk to him," Rika said. At Jayce's nod, she released his hand reluctantly and went to stand beside Sionnach. In a very low voice, she told the faery, "Maili's in need of a few reminders of her place . . ."

"No courts out here, princess," Sionnach murmured softly enough that Jayce wouldn't hear. "Rule of strength or influence."

She growled a little and said, "They're acting like animals." She reached up to check the injuries on his face, touching him as she only did when he'd come to her injured and seeking help. "That's my fault. . . . I'm—"

"Shhh." Sionnach stepped away, leaving Rika with one hand still in the air, and turned his attention to Jayce. "So . . . Jayce, right?"

Jayce nodded. "And you're . . . ?"

"Sionnach," he said, drawing out the word so it sounded like "shhh knock." The faery circled Jayce, not looking very human. He leaned in behind Jayce and sniffed him. "If it's easier, you can call me 'Shy.'"

"Thanks for the help at the club, Sionnach," Jayce said levelly.

Jayce either didn't notice or didn't care that Sionnach had just sniffed him. Rika had spent enough time with Jayce that she couldn't say she was completely surprised by how well he'd reacted to everything so far; he was naturally mellow. But Rika didn't like Sionnach acting more like an animal than a human. He wasn't even playing at being one of them right now; he *could* act like a human. She'd seen it, but right now, he was acting like himself. Seeing him around Jayce, being so much the solitary faery, made Rika remind herself that he *was* all faery; he wasn't someone she should trust. He was and had always been a faery, one with motivations she'd never wanted to understand—and still didn't.

She scowled at him, thinking back on his earlier visit,

when he had so casually told her that he knew that Jayce was in danger and that he'd done nothing about it.

However, Sionnach was well accustomed to her censure after several decades of their friendship. He merely folded his arms and gave her a wide smile. He sniffed Jayce again.

"Stop it, Sionnach." Rika stepped between them and took Jayce's hand. Then, she walked toward the same pallet where she'd been sitting when Sionnach had visited earlier and sat, tugging Jayce down beside her in the process.

Jayce looked a bit amused, no longer seeming as perplexed as when they'd first arrived or as awed as when they were in the tunnel. He leaned back against the wall, stretched his long legs out in front of him, and then looked from her to Sionnach and back again. "You're both a little unusual."

"Quite," Sionnach said, and then he laughed.

Rika knew him well enough to understand that he approved of how Jayce was responding to the situation. A lot of people would be freaking out over her cave home, the fight, the speed at which they'd moved, and Sionnach's odd behavior. Jayce wasn't. Still, Rika told Sionnach, "I can't ask him to stay here."

"I don't mind," Jayce said softly from beside her. "I'd like to spend more time with you."

Rika glanced at him, but didn't speak. She *couldn't.* The flare of happiness inside of her threatened to make her sound like even more of a fool than she probably already had. By all rights, Jayce should be fleeing. He should be trying to escape her, wondering if she was crazed and dangerous. She didn't understand why he wasn't, and she wasn't sure she wanted to ask.

Still staring at her, Jayce added, "I can go get my gear and—"

In an almost human-like walk, Sionnach went to a shadowed edge of the room. When he retrieved a rucksack and bedroll and dropped them on the ground in front of Rika and Jayce, they broke their locked gaze and looked at Sionnach instead.

"How? Where? . . . Never mind." Jayce smiled wryly and shook his head. "I'm guessing you're part of the I-can't-answer-questions team."

"Oh, I'll tell you anything you want to know. Ask away." Sionnach sounded somewhere between amused and malicious, and Rika wondered what game he was playing at.

After a tension-filled pause, Jayce asked, "Anything?"

With a speed too quick to truly appear human, Rika stood and snatched hold of Sionnach's arm. "Move, Shy. *Now.*"

She pulled him away from Jayce, toward the door, so they could speak in relative privacy.

"Oh my . . . Are *you* asking *me* to keep secrets, princess?" He widened his eyes, but his tone was very serious, and Rika was reminded yet again that he had always been a faery. "Are you telling me that it's okay to keep secrets from those we care about?"

There were layers of meanings under his words that she couldn't begin to fathom. The tension had grown thick, but

Rika couldn't decide if it was anger or something else that was driving the fox faery. She released his arm. If she were any other faery in the desert, Sionnach would've reacted as if she'd just challenged his authority.

"Rika?" he prompted. His gaze told her there were more things hidden in his words than she knew. She wasn't sure, though, what he was thinking as he waited for her reply—any more than she was sure what her reply was.

Do I think keeping secrets is okay? That was his question. She simply wasn't sure why her answer mattered to Sionnach, but it was apparent that it did. To some degree she had to believe that it was okay to keep secrets. Elsewise, she would have to tell Jayce how often she'd watched him. She rolled the question over in her mind. There was no way the fox faery meant it to be purely a question about her and Jayce. She knew that much at least.

Behind her, she heard movement, and glanced back as Jayce stood and grabbed his things from where Sionnach had deposited them. He started toward the entrance to the cave. "You two obviously have something to sort out, so I can—"

"Please don't go." Stricken, Rika stepped farther away from Sionnach and shot a plaintive glance at him, wordlessly asking him to be less . . . him, less fey.

"She wants *you* here." Sionnach stepped in front of Jayce. "I took care of what needed taken care of so you could be here with Rika. Don't waste this chance."

And then he left the cave.

Rika was utterly motionless for a moment, Jayce on one

side, Sionnach outside the cave opening. She was confused by Sionnach's help, by his actions here tonight, and by the way he'd seemingly helped push Jayce toward her while saying such things that made her wonder if she really knew the fox faery at all.

Carefully, she touched Jayce's forearm. "Please stay here for a minute. I need to talk to him, but I'll be right back." She swallowed nervously and then added in a rush, "I really want you to stay . . . not just for your safety, but because . . . I *want* you here. He's my friend though, and I need to find out what happened, and he doesn't want to talk in front of you. Please just give me a minute."

After a moment, Jayce sighed and said, "Why not?" Then he walked toward one of the tunnels with his bag without saying anything else.

As soon as Jayce disappeared into the tunnels, Rika ran outside and found Sionnach staring at the desert. He'd slid to the far side of the ledge in front of her cave, precariously perched so he wasn't visible from inside, and Rika wondered briefly if he'd stood out here like this when she was unaware of it. Right now, that wouldn't surprise her.

"What did you do to get his things?" Rika demanded in a whisper.

"Nothing special." Then in a blink Sionnach suddenly looked like Jayce, but still dressed in his own clothing. "Just a simple glamour, princess. You might only use them to stay hidden, but there's a world of possibilities. I stopped at Jayce's house before I came out here so I could explain to

Jayce's father that I'd be off camping with Del . . . and then stopped and told Del I'd met the girl of my dreams and was going to see her."

Rika blushed. "I'm not—"

Sionnach was still wearing Jayce's face as he said, "The girl of my dreams? You are. You're one of the most amazing"—he pulled her into his arms, holding her in a position appropriate for slow dancing or kissing—"gorgeous"—he stroked her hair—"unusual girls I've ever met. Who wouldn't want to hide away with you?"

When Rika didn't reply, Sionnach leaned in like he was going to kiss her. "And you believe in me enough that you aren't seeing through the glamour . . . or are you seeing the real me right now, Rika?"

Rika remained immobile in his embrace. Her hands were on his upper chest, and that was all that kept any distance between them. Then, she said his name, half question she didn't want answered and half answer to the question he'd posed. "Shy?"

The glamour faded, and Sionnach looked at her from his own face. He kissed her nose, a strangely innocent act after the hungry way he'd just been looking at her. "I'll be back in a few days, princess. Go see Jayce."

By the time Rika could begin to figure out what to say, Sionnach was gone. If someone had told her yesterday that the mortal she was half in love with and the faery she considered an almost friend would both say such outrageous things to her on the same day, she would've laughed madly.

Sure, Sionnach flirted now and again, but he'd never truly intimated that he considered her more than a distraction to tease. They'd spoken often of the desert, of courts and politics, of plants and weather. He hadn't acted like *that* with her, and Jayce . . . well, he hadn't known she existed.

The world had gone off-kilter, and she wasn't quite sure what to think. All she could do tonight was take advantage of the unexpected opportunity to talk to Jayce when he was able to see her, when he could actually reply to her. Nervously, she walked deeper into the cave and followed the tunnel back to the cavern where her mural was. Jayce was staring at it with something like wonder on his face.

She came up beside him.

He didn't look away from the art. "You're incredible."

"I'm not."

Then, he did look at her, and they were face-to-face, with very little distance between them. Unlike Sionnach, Jayce seemed as nervous as Rika felt. Strangely, that made her feel more comfortable.

"This is the weirdest day of my life." Jayce stepped even nearer, but it was only one step. His actions grew more tentative with each breath. "And one of the best."

Rika stayed still, caught between wondering whether it was better to act or react. One of his hands curled around her waist; his fingers rested on the small of her back. His embrace was about keeping her close, holding her near to his chest, lining their bodies up. But that was it—the promise, the temptation, and no more. The tension in his muscles made clear that he was debating moving closer.

He went so far as to tilt his head as if he'd kiss her.

Rika waited, counting the beats of her heart as if by counting she could slow the furious rhythm.

After being utterly untouched for years, she was in someone's arms for the second time in mere moments—and yet she was still unkissed.

Is it me? She licked her lips, trying to find the words to ask such an unpleasant question. *Am I . . . What, though? Unattractive? Uninteresting? Unpleasant in some way?*

He ducked his head then, dropping his gaze. "I'm afraid."

"Afraid?" Her voice was soft and girly, and she hated the way it sounded, the way she felt. After so long, she shouldn't be this meek.

He nodded.

"Of what?"

"You. Me. All the things that aren't making any sense . . ." His words weren't much more than a whisper.

"I can't explain *all* of that, but—"

"I still want to be here, to be with you." His voice was so low that if he pulled away, she wasn't sure she'd hear what he was saying. He didn't let go of her; he stayed kissably close, waiting for her, giving her the choice to decide what happened next.

"I want you here too." She flattened her palms against his chest. Under the skin, his heart was racing, beating as rapidly as hers was. In this, they were well matched—except her pulse raced with excitement and his with fear.

"You live in a cave, Rika."

"I do."

He hesitated even longer before speaking this time. Haltingly, he asked, "Is he . . . Sionnach, is he your . . . something?"

Rika hesitated, not knowing the answer as clearly as she did yesterday. All she could say of what she did know was: "Sometimes I think he's my friend, but I'm not always sure."

Jayce nodded.

"I don't know if it's the weirdness or you saving me or . . ." His words faded, and he took a shuddering breath. "I know I should step back and think because I'm pretty sure that getting tangled up with you is risky. You were in a fight tonight, and we ran faster than is possible, and . . . you live in a cave."

"I know."

"I want to know you." He paused. "If I stay, will you answer any of my questions?"

She didn't know what to say. She was bound by rules, and she couldn't break them without either consequences or permission. Jayce was appealing enough to make her consider it, but she would prefer another solution—one that didn't involve him knowing what she was. She wasn't looking for forever. Forever wasn't something she intended to ever seek again. What she wanted was something brief, intense, real for a while. She wanted to burn up under the wanting. If she were a modern girl, a mortal girl from his time, she'd lean up and kiss him, solve the dilemma.

After a moment, she whispered, "Just kiss me. It doesn't have to lead to anything. Just a kiss."

Jayce brushed his closed lips against hers. It wasn't enough. After so long being alone, after watching him and loving him in the only way she knew how, she was finally in his arms and all she wanted was the kiss she'd dreamed of in secrecy. He wasn't giving her that, so she broke the rules. She said, "I'm not human, but I used to be a very long time ago."

And then she decided to try out this modern-girl thing: she kissed him thoroughly before he could answer.

Chapter 8

After their kiss, Jayce had asked her to explain what she meant, but she couldn't, not really. "I need to get permission to say any more," she'd told him. Jayce went back to town, and Rika set out to find Sionnach, realizing that this would be the first time she went to her Alpha with a request. It rankled, and she pondered what she'd do if Sionnach said no.

Do I want this enough to challenge him?

She wasn't sure. All she could say for certain was that while she wasn't sure of the rules for courtship in this modern world, she was pretty sure that lying wasn't a good plan. So she needed to seek Sionnach's permission.

She found the fox faery nestled in the shadows of a rocky edge that formed the side of what would become a water hole in the wet season. He wouldn't be visible if she hadn't wound her way through the canyon and through a narrow opening. He didn't quite flinch at her appearance, but he didn't offer her a smile either. All he said was "Princess."

Rika smothered a sigh. He didn't often sink into melancholy moods—or if he did, she hadn't seen many of them—so she was at a momentary loss. Carefully, she skirted the cacti that flourished here and walked over to stand awkwardly in front of him. "Why do you call me that?"

He shrugged. "You weren't the queen of winter or summer, but you could've been. You aren't the Alpha, but you could be . . . so, princess."

She sat down next to him on the ground. "I never wanted to be a queen or Alpha. I just wanted to be loved."

Sionnach stared at her for long enough that she squirmed. They had discussed her past enough that he shouldn't be surprised by her words. Maybe it was his mood, or maybe it was because he'd almost kissed her. Either way, she felt uncharacteristically vulnerable.

"Shy?"

"You like the mortal," Sionnach said.

"Yes."

"That's why you're here." He looked away from her to stare out at the desert.

Rika frowned. Sionnach had all but shoved Jayce into her arms, yet now he was looking at her like she was wrong to have done exactly what he seemed to want. Cautiously, she said, "I won't tell him what I am if you forbid it."

The fox faery nodded, but he didn't look at her. "Do you remember when we met?"

She smiled. "You were dancing in the moonlight like you

didn't know anyone was around."

"I knew you were there." He glanced at her. "I knew you were there every time before that too. I thought maybe if I waited you'd come out of your prison and join me. I wanted you to love the desert like I do. I wanted you to be happy here."

"I am. Now."

"Because of the mortal?"

Rika nodded.

"If I say no, will you challenge me?" Sionnach asked. His voice was more cautious than she'd ever heard.

"You're my friend."

"Is that a no?"

Rika still didn't have an answer to that question. She'd thought about it, but she had no desire to be in power. That wasn't her goal. All she wanted was happiness. She settled on saying, "I don't want to fight you."

"You'd win." Sionnach flashed her one of his mischievous smiles. "We both know that."

"You'd leave the desert if you weren't Alpha," she half said, half asked.

Sionnach shrugged, neither agreeing with her nor denying her claim. He picked up a rock and tossed it into the distance. They both watched it hit the ground before he stood and brushed the sand from his legs. He glanced down at her. "You should tell him what you are. I'll do the same." He touched his misshapen ears. "I suspect the look of me without a glamour will convince him faster than anything you say."

Rika came to her feet and impulsively hugged Sionnach. "You're a good friend."

"Not always," he murmured.

She laughed. "For a faery, you're amazing."

He said nothing as he walked toward the gap in the rocks that would lead to the more open desert. He stayed silent as they walked toward Silver Ridge. It was only when they were almost at the town that he stopped her with a hand on her arm and said, "Don't forget that *you* are fey too."

At that, Rika stared at him, mouth open but no words coming to her lips. She knew what she was: she'd been mortal for less than two decades and faery for much longer. She wanted to argue with him, but all of her words were close enough to lies that they dried up before she could utter them.

"You have held yourself apart from us for years, Rika. Tell your mortal what you are, but stop hiding yourself away from the fey who live here." Then Sionnach gestured back at the land they'd just crossed. "Bring him to your den, princess. I'll be there to help him believe you."

Rika was silent as he turned and fled. She knew that her insistence on seclusion frustrated him, but she hadn't realized just how much until that moment. She'd been separate from the faeries in both the Winter Court and Summer Court, and they'd seemed to prefer it. Since she'd been in the desert, she'd assumed that the faeries here wanted the same thing, that her origin as something else bothered them. Faeries had a long history of treating mortals like playthings, sometimes like beloved toys but more often like things that could be discarded or broken. She'd watched them knock Jayce to what could have been serious injury only yesterday. She wasn't like that—or okay with it.

Still pondering the things Sionnach had said, and trying not to think about things he had left unsaid, she walked through town until she found Jayce. He was sitting with Del and Kayley, and they all seemed to be having a loud discussion about the best way to reach a petroglyph site. When Jayce saw her, he smiled.

When she was near enough that only he would hear, she leaned in and whispered, "I can answer those questions if you want."

He leaned back to look into her eyes. "When?"

"Now."

At that, he stood and told his friends, "I'm out."

Del's expression wasn't friendly. "Too good to be around—"

"Stop," Kayley hissed at him. She flashed a smile at Rika and said, "Sorry."

"We'll be back," Jayce offered. "We just need to talk."

Kayley nodded, and Del made a shooing motion with his hand. "Go."

When they reached the open desert, Rika took his hand in hers and reminded him, "Remember to run."

Then they raced across the desert as they had when she'd taken him to her home the first time. It was an unsettling feeling, as if the ground didn't quite exist but was instead almost like water. He felt his feet touch and slide, but it wasn't the same as stepping on solid surface. He couldn't decide if he liked it or found it frightening. What he did know was that it was different. *She* was different, and out here where the world was a vast expanse of the same thing, different was extra exciting. He loved the desert, the way the sky seemed to stretch out endlessly and the air sometimes seemed to leave a trace of a taste on his lips. He loved the fierce and sometimes odd creatures that thrived in what some would call an unfriendly land. None of that changed the fact that he'd lived here his whole life and was excited by the prospect of someone unusual.

They reached the cave where she lived, and he stiffened at the sight of her friend Sionnach, who sat on a small ledge, kicking his feet like a child and watching them with an unreadable expression. He'd obviously seen their approach, but he made no move to greet them.

"Shy," Rika said, her tone holding something of both a greeting and a warning.

He flashed teeth at them in a smile that didn't look very friendly, and Jayce tensed. He'd thought that the two were friends, but right now, he wondered if they'd argued or he'd misunderstood their friendship. He stepped closer to Rika. Sure, she'd more than held her own in the fight at Dead Ends, but for some reason, Sionnach seemed more menacing than that group.

For a fraction of a moment, Jayce could have sworn that Sionnach's ears were pointed and—disturbingly—that he had a fluffy fox tail that flicked to the side. He blinked to try to clear his eyes, thinking maybe he had sand in them and it was messing with his vision.

"Something wrong?" Sionnach said in a teasing voice.

"Shy!" This time Rika definitely sounded like she was warning him.

"Seeing things maybe?"

Jayce looked at Rika and then down at his ankles. "Maybe I was bitten." He lifted one foot and looked at his hiking boots. There were no holes where something could have gotten to his skin. He didn't feel like he had heat stroke, so he suspected he wasn't hallucinating. He looked back at Sionnach, who was now standing at the mouth of the cave.

Rika sighed while staring at Sionnach, and then she looked at Jayce. "You're not seeing things." She motioned toward the rocks. "Climb up. We can talk inside."

Mutely Jayce did as she asked. Sionnach was standing inside the cave, his back against the wall and body angled to the side. It was dim enough that Jayce couldn't look at his ears without going over close to him. He didn't need to do that though because in the next moment, Sionnach said, "I'm not human."

He pushed his hair away from his ears, revealing pointed tips. He flashed his teeth at Jayce again, showing sharper-than-normal incisors. Finally, he stared at Jayce as he flicked his tail forward.

Jayce didn't fall to the ground in shock, but he did lower himself to the cave floor. "Huh."

"I'm not either." Rika's voice was soft, but it still felt loud in the silence that followed Sionnach's little show. "I used to be. I told you that."

"I thought it was, I don't know, a *metaphor* or something." Jayce looked from her to the guy with the fox tail and back. "Do you have a tail too?"

"No." She folded her arms over her chest. "I was human, like you."

"And now you're . . . what?"

"Faeries," Sionnach answered. "We live for pretty much ever, and we have some traits that are different."

"I thought faeries were little winged—"

"No," Sionnach all but snarled. "We're not the things of children's stories. I don't know when that rumor started, but we're not going to throw glitter at you and simper. We're the things that nightmares—"

"Shy," Rika cut him off. She sighed and walked closer to Jayce. Cautiously, like she expected him to flee, she sat down beside him. "There *are* faeries who are frightening, but not all of us. I don't mean you any harm. I *like* you, and I hope you still want to . . . be around me now that you know."

Jayce looked at her and then at Sionnach. Some part of his mind wanted to explain this away, to have an answer that proved that they were messing with him. The rest of him realized that this was real. He was talking to creatures that shouldn't exist. He wasn't afraid, though. Mostly, he was fascinated.

"So why didn't I see the tail before?"

"Glamour. We can hide our true appearances from mortals, or"—Sionnach vanished and then reappeared crouching down beside Jayce a moment later—"hide from you completely."

"Whoa!"

Sionnach laughed, turned away, waved over his shoulder, and then vanished again.

"Is he still here? Can *you* see him?" Jayce asked quietly.

"I can. Faeries can." She smiled nervously before adding, "But he's gone now. It's just us. Is that okay?"

Jayce reached out and traced her cheek with his fingertips. "I'm alone with the girl I like who happens to be even cooler than I already thought. It's very okay." He leaned closer and kissed her. He'd known she was different, but he couldn't have guessed she was this unusual. He was kissing a faery. The thought made him pull back and grin at her. "This is awesome."

Chapter 9

For the next two weeks, the desert fey were quiet. Sionnach had called in what favors he could to assure that Rika had time alone with her mortal boy. Seeing her come out of her shell to be romanced by the human boy was exactly what Sionnach had planned, but as he'd watched them smile tentatively at each other, his heart hurt at the sight—enough that he'd increasingly sought comfort in a mortal as well. He'd let himself grow closer to Carissa, although he'd almost called her the wrong name more than once.

But the more time he'd spent with her, the more Sionnach realized that she was nothing like Rika. The two shared the same tiny stature, but Carissa was lighthearted where Rika was serious. Carissa was quick to laughter, teasing as if she were fey, happy to dance in the middle of the desert. There were no long-carried sorrows in his Carissa, and as the days passed, Sionnach had lost himself a little more in her affection. At first, he thought only to distract himself, but as time passed, he remembered why he had enjoyed frolicking with mortals: there was something pure in the lives of the finite.

Sionnach found himself temporarily enchanted by the girl with whom he spent his days. Today, though, he was interrupted before he could reach his evening date with the mortal girl. Maili had waited in the shadows. She stalked toward him, looking like something darker than should be in his town. At Maili's feet a mortal teen lay facedown on the ground. One arm was flung out so the fingertips were in the edge of a puddle. The streetlight at the end of the alley cast enough light to illuminate the blood that the boy had lost. The mortal was either unconscious or dead.

"You need to rein it in," Sionnach said warningly. "I've been patient."

"I get bored, *Shy*. Before you got so close to someone who used to be one of *them*"—she wrinkled her nose like she smelled something unpleasant—"you used to understand that."

"Things change." He was so tense that his tail flicked to the side. He didn't bother pointing out that Rika had been fey far longer than she'd been mortal. Mildly, he added, "People change; faeries change."

"Not us. Not *real* faeries."

"Even us, Maili."

"Not all of us." She took a step away from him, tucking one hand behind her back at the waistband of her pants, where he knew a weapon was undoubtedly hidden.

"We are strong, and *they* are disposable. They don't matter."

"Mortals matter." As he looked at Maili, he tilted his head as if his animal nature would let him see what she still hid. There was something more to see here. This scene was too carefully constructed for it to be about a dead or injured boy.

"They shouldn't, not to us," Maili insisted.

"If we want to survive in the world today—" Sionnach stopped midsentence, caught by the sight of a silhouette at the end of the alley. He didn't need to turn around to see that the person peering into the shadows was Carissa.

He knew that the alley looked deserted to Carissa; she couldn't see him or Maili. She *would* see the body if not for the fact that Sionnach hurriedly crouched down and touched the boy's arm to extend his own invisibility over the fallen mortal. In touching him, Sionnach knew that he was dead.

"Sionnach?" Carissa called. "Are you here? I got your message."

He didn't answer, and Maili grinned cruelly. Two of her lackeys came to stand on either side of the mortal girl. Carissa didn't see them either. She was a pawn to Maili, nothing more than an object to force his hand. The boy was killed to set the stage, to clarify the threat to Carissa that Maili wanted Sionnach to understand.

Sionnach didn't move away from the boy; he couldn't without revealing him. His tail flicked wildly as he ordered,

"You've made your point. Leave her alone."

"For tonight," Maili agreed. "But I haven't made my point, not yet."

He felt the wound that followed her words almost before he realized what was happening. Maili swung her arm up and slashed across Sionnach's chest with her carved bone knife.

"They are a distraction, Sionnach. You were so busy watching her and hiding him that you didn't see the real danger, the danger to a *faery*." Maili unwrapped a rusty iron quad-pronged thing, and before he could reply, she jabbed it into his stomach. "Faeries have no business worrying about mortals."

Maili didn't pull the weapon out of his stomach. She just let go. Sionnach stared at it, trying to determine the best next step. The pain was excruciating enough that he felt separate from himself, as if he weren't exactly anchored within his body.

Maili swallowed audibly before she said, "Power, strength, that's what gives you voice. You are weakening because of her, because of Rika's influence."

There was no help for it. Sionnach fell, but he didn't crumple or cry out. He hadn't become Alpha in this territory without learning to hide his pain. In a sort of slow-motion tilt, he let himself fall back against the wall, and then he slid down so he was reclining in the dirty street. "That was really foolish."

"Smart, actually. It's iron, Sionnach. Rusty bits of poison just broke off inside your body. The others will see you like this, an example of what happens when I'm not obeyed." Maili sounded weak, shivery with either the pain of her own contact with the iron or the fear of what she had just done. She glanced at her hand. In that brief contact, it was already bruised and had raised welts from gripping the vile metal. "You've forgotten what you are, and I need you out of my way."

"I know exactly what I am." Sionnach slid the weapon out of his stomach. He didn't fling it away; instead he dropped it in the puddle beside him. He didn't want to have it tucked between his body and his hand, but he had no other weapon. He'd keep this one near him in case he needed it. Pointedly, he looked from her injured hand to his own. His hand was barely bruised by touching the handle. He was stronger, and they both knew it.

"Think about this," he cautioned her.

"I have. Rule of might: I have it, and you're losing it." Maili's expression was anxious, but she squared her shoulders before adding, "I just need a chance to prove I'm strong enough to be Alpha. You were in the way."

"You're making a mistake." Sionnach glanced at the mouth of the alley. Several of Carissa's friends that he hadn't yet met had just joined her. Despite the worried look on her face, she was safer now, and he was relieved. Right now, he didn't think Maili would harm her; her goal seemed to have been merely to use her to distract him, to make him look away. It had worked. Nonetheless, he was glad Carissa wasn't alone now—and therefore not as vulnerable.

Maili squatted beside him, glaring. "You are no better than us, fox."

"Maybe not better, but I *am* smarter. Rika won't forgive this, and she's stronger than all of us."

Maili laughed. "Power is only valuable if you use it. Rika doesn't."

In silence, Sionnach watched Carissa walk away with her friends. He wished he could tell her that he hadn't sent a message and then abandoned her, but there were more important things than a few moments of her worry. Being Alpha in the desert meant that he had to put security and order in front of his own interests. Alpha was a duty, one that he sometimes wished he could hand to another faery—not forever, but for a few years so he could enjoy life more. It had been far too long since he'd had a true holiday.

Maili didn't understand what being Alpha meant. She saw being Alpha as a thing of power. It wasn't. It was a responsibility, and the only reason Rika hadn't claimed it was because she hadn't had someone to protect or defend. Now that she had Jayce, she was more likely to be receptive. That had been his original plan. Now that Sionnach had been poisoned with a toxic weapon, Rika had another reason to step forward.

Maybe I should've just gotten myself stabbed instead of finding her a date. He wasn't quite sure which of the two had caused more pain. He closed his eyes with a laugh at his own expense.

Chapter 10

Since the day she'd kissed Jayce, Rika had been happier than she'd thought possible. He was with her as a real part of her life, and the faeries in the desert had been leaving them alone since that odd night at Dead Ends. She knew Sionnach was responsible for that, but he acted like it was the most normal thing in the world to help her navigate the difficulties of dating a mortal while keeping him safe from meddling faeries.

Today, Rika walked through town visibly with Jayce's arm around her. Maybe Jayce was what she'd been waiting for all this time. She could finally have a relationship. When she'd "dated" Keenan, it had been a different century, and the Summer King hadn't ever kissed her with the sort of fervor Jayce now did. Keenan had never touched her without ulterior motivation, but Jayce . . . he was different. When he pulled her into his arms, he wasn't trying to convince her to sacrifice anything, wasn't trying to hide his true intentions from her. Jayce's only interest seemed to be making her forget the world around them—and *that* was an interest she could happily support.

Being with him, being out around people, made her realize how much of *living* she'd been missing. She wanted more of it, the silly jokes and the casual touches. She wanted to spend days doing nothing but kissing. She wanted to be lost to the dizzying joy of touch. What Jayce wanted, however, was more talking.

"I want to know you better," he repeated. "It was a sentence he'd used far too often, one that hinted at more than she could offer right now.

"You *do* know me. We've spent hours talking and—"

"Are you happy being with me?"

She paused. If there was a right way to say that she was happier than when she had watched him in secret, she didn't know it. Instead, she said, "I never expected to get to touch you. I didn't think I'd become this . . . I don't know . . . *free*."

"Free enough to answer more questions?" His voice sounded teasing, and his fingers trailed over her arm.

If Rika had only her desires to consider, they'd spend more time touching and less time talking, but she knew she was being unfair. She'd had time to learn about him before he knew she existed. Still, she let herself simply enjoy his caress for a moment more before asking, "What else do you need to know?"

"Everything. What you did before we met." Jayce stepped away, clearing his throat briefly as if the temptation was more than he wanted. "I just want to know everything about you, your world, your history. *Everything*."

She knew he suspected there were plenty of things she hadn't told him—especially when she slipped and commented on things she wouldn't know since they'd only just begun dating. The times they spent together, unbeknownst to him, had taught her so much about him. She'd already felt like she'd known him so well . . . at least, she had thought so until he took her into his arms. Then she realized that there was this entire part of him she couldn't have known until now.

When Rika thought about her life, about memories she'd tried for years to ignore, there was nothing in her remembrances that she wanted to share with Jayce. She'd made a bad choice, and she'd suffered for it until the next girl made that same foolish choice. Then she'd hidden herself away until a strange fox faery slowly lulled her into friendship. These were not memories she wanted to share—or even have.

As calmly as she could, she told Jayce, "*Nothing* about the past makes me happy. It's now that matters. Who cares about what happened then?"

When only silence met her words, Rika wondered if she needed to say more, but then he brushed his lips over hers.

"It's *good* that I want to know everything about you." He offered her a teasing smile. "You really *aren't* good at the dating thing, are you?"

"Well, I've only done it one other time." She tried to match his playful tone, but failed. So she kissed him and then added, "And he wasn't as exciting as you. He was just a jerk of a faery."

"Right. I'm more fun than a faery."

"He didn't want *me*, Jayce," she said quietly. "And the person he pretended to be wasn't real. I wasn't a person to him; I was a game."

"Then he was a fool." Jayce rested his forehead against hers. Their bodies touched, and in the way he had of making things seem better with the right words and gentle caresses, he eased the shadows she was trying to forget. "Don't make everyone suffer because of it."

Rika stepped away from him, trying to think of the words to give him what he sought without surrendering her past. "I'm trying not to. I'm happy *now*. I made some mistakes; then, I came to the desert trying to forget them. Now, I'm with you. The rest doesn't matter."

"Sooner or later, it will. I want to be with you. That means I need to understand your world." Jayce took her hand.

"*This* is my world too," Rika objected. "I wish it was the only one. . . ."

He tugged her forward, but instead of continuing the conversation, he resorted to the only thing other than kisses guaranteed to make her smile. "Art fix?"

"Art fix," she echoed. "Did you find something new? Where? Did *you* do it? We could run if you tell me where."

He laughed. "Patient one," he teased. "It's just this way. Let's walk."

They walked along the street for a short distance, and then turned into a shadowy alley. Graffiti decorated the side of the buildings—intricate murals and abstract sketches, faces and artists' tags.

Rika leaned her head on Jayce's shoulder and looked up. "Good dimensions with the reds . . ."

"Too busy," Jayce rebutted.

"Minimalist." She mock sighed.

"The simple things are best." He kissed her.

When he pulled away, she gave him a look of adoration. "Good argument."

Then she looked back at the graffiti, smiling and leaning close to Jayce. They stayed together for several moments, and she marveled again at how much these past few weeks had meant to her. After long years where no one touched her in affection, now she felt like the span of minutes between caresses was too long.

Jayce motioned toward an opening between buildings, not quite an alley but more of a passageway. "Cut through here."

They wound their way through it to a wider passage and then one alley and a second. Together, they crossed a small street, Jayce leading. Rika trailed behind him, holding his hand as they stepped into a third alley.

When she saw the ground, saw the body there, she yanked her hand free and ran. "No!"

"What?"

Jayce couldn't see because he had only human sight, but there, unconscious on the ground, was Sionnach. He was the only faery in the desert that she'd called a friend, and he was bleeding on the ground.

She dropped to the ground and reached out to see if Sionnach was alive.

As she touched his arm, he became visible to Jayce as well.

Jayce dropped to his knees beside her, looking as shocked as she felt, and she wished now that she *could* shelter him from her world. Seeing bloodied bodies appearing out of the air was understandably startling; the ugly part of Rika's world—the part where violence was not rare—wasn't something she'd ever planned to share with Jayce.

He looked like he might be sick for a moment, but then he swallowed and asked, "Is he alive?"

"Yes. He's alive still." As she examined Sionnach, her hand brushed the weapon, still dirty with Sionnach's blood. She recoiled in pain and disgust. "Iron."

Jayce glanced at the weapon she was carefully not touching now.

"Can you pick it up so I can have someone get the . . . scent from it later? To track who did this?" She knew she was blushing, as if the faeries' more natural animal traits were embarrassing. This, too, she would rather have not shared with him.

Silently, Jayce pulled a bandana from his satchel and wrapped the bloody weapon in it. His gaze darted worriedly at Sionnach, as he tucked the weapon into his satchel. Later, Rika would need to talk to Jayce about how attacks were handled in the world of solitary faeries—or hope that he didn't ask questions she wanted to avoid answering. For now, though, she was simply grateful that he was willing to help her and that she didn't have to touch the noxious weapon.

Rika opened Sionnach's shirt and held it away from his stomach. The gouges in his stomach were inflamed, swollen, and angry.

Sionnach moaned as she prodded the injuries, and she tried to examine him without letting her own whimpers or cries of fury out. There would be time enough for temper later. Right now, she needed to be strong.

In his state of weakness, Sionnach's fox-ish traits were more obvious. His features were sharper, cheeks more defined, tail obvious, and the tips of his pointed ears visible. He looked more faery than she ever would.

"Where do you go when one of you are hurt. . . . I mean . . . You can't take him to the hospital, right?" Jayce stepped back from them, near but obviously not knowing quite what to do. "I want to help. Tell me how."

"In the courts, there are healers. Here"—she pulled Sionnach's shirt farther up, and she could see the slash was partially healed—"Shy will make do with my care. I need to move him."

"Is he going to be—"

"He'll be *fine*." Rika looked up as soon as the words left her lips and offered Jayce a contrite smile to soften the harsh tone of her words. "But she won't."

"She?"

"There's only one faery stupid enough to injure Shy. Maili's going to find out how very idiotic that was." Rika paused and glanced at Jayce, needing him to understand that she wasn't a monster. "I'll check first. Either Shy will wake and tell me or I'll have someone scent the weapon."

Jayce nodded.

Rika lifted Sionnach and cradled him in her arms as if he were a small child. His head lolled back, and the fear she was trying to ignore grew. *Faeries are resilient*, she reminded herself. Sionnach had stood against attacker after challenger after troublemaker in the years she'd known him. Being Alpha in the desert was not without its difficulties. The difference this time was in the treachery of the assault. Striking another faery with iron wasn't done lightly—or forgiven easily. Either Sionnach or Rika would have to discipline the faery, make clear that such assaults could not happen in the desert, and they'd need to do so with enough force that no one else would attempt to do so again. First, though, she needed to remove the poison from Sionnach's flesh.

He'll heal. He has to.

More steadily than she expected, she told Jayce, "I need to go."

She wasn't sure if it was the fear she was failing to hide or the anger that floated just under that fear; either way, Jayce looked even more worried.

"Should I follow?" he asked.

Rika shook her head. "No. Not right now. Tomorrow. I'll come get you if I can leave him alone long enough. . . ." She paused. "Do you have your phone?"

"Yeah . . ." Jayce pulled it out. "Who do you need me—"

"Call Del. Go be with him," she interrupted. "Even if it wasn't her that did this, Maili is dangerous, and Shy is too injured to enforce rules. You need to go where you're safe. She won't approach a group. Witnesses can cause trouble with the faery courts. She'll avoid that. Stay near lots of steel. Faeries can't abide iron or steel." Her gaze dropped to Sionnach, his injury proof of how badly the toxic metals could wound a faery.

Jayce hesitated, as if he would speak but wasn't sure if he should.

"Please? I need to get him to safety, but . . ." Rika wanted to let him know that he was something rare and precious, that his safety mattered to her more than he could know, but she wasn't sure of the words, and she'd already asked him to accept things far more quickly than he'd liked. He was trying to understand her world, but it wasn't easy.

"If Maili hurt you, it'd destroy me," Rika said. "If you . . . I *need* you safe, and I don't trust that you are if you are alone."

"Sure," he agreed. "You be careful too, okay?"

"I'll come to you as soon as I can. . . . I need to get him home and remove the poison," she tried to be careful with her words. "I can't take you both, and it's not safe for you to follow me on your own, and I can't let Del know where I live, and—"

"It's okay," Jayce interrupted. "Go."

She nodded as she faded to invisibility with Sionnach in her arms and began to run home with the unconscious faery held tightly in her arms.

Chapter 11

Rika wasn't sure how long it took to get Sionnach to the safety of her cave, nor was she certain how many faeries saw her carrying him across the desert. She knew it was best to hide his injured state, but trying to find a stealthy way across the openness of the desert wasn't an option. If anyone were foolish enough to further threaten the faery in her arms, she'd deal with them. Being remade as a faery strong enough to hold the weight of winter inside her skin meant that Rika—like every other former Winter Girl—was stronger than most any solitary faery. She'd never used that strength to assert dominance in the desert, never felt the need to do so, but she was willing to do so now. She'd thought she'd surrendered the anger she'd felt over Maili's behavior on the cliff and in the club a couple of weeks ago. She'd written it off as faery posturing, but now that she was lowering an unconscious faery to her bed, she wasn't feeling anywhere near forgiving.

The bed upon which she'd lowered Sionnach was nothing more than a pile of various blankets and furs. Furs weren't truly the sort of thing that made sense in the desert, but she'd never had reason to explain it to another faery. Her bed made her feel comfortable because of its familiarity; it was an admitted result of having lived in a simple home both as a mortal and as a Winter Girl.

Sionnach hadn't opened his eyes yet. Despite the jarring journey across the desert, he remained silent and unconscious now even as he rolled restlessly.

Rika started a fire. It wasn't the first time she'd tended his injuries, but familiarity with the process didn't make it any more palatable.

She filled a basin with water and cleaned away the blood and dirt. The skin around the wounds was already hot to the touch, and a fever had begun to consume him. She soaked a cloth in the water, tried to cool his feverish skin, and hoped that the fox faery's body would begin to push the metal out. Time and again, she put ice-cold water on Sionnach until the fever let up a bit. Time and again, she poured the red-tinged water into a crack in the cave floor where it would vanish into the depths below her.

"Wake up, Shy," she ordered.

The bits of metal that had broken off the rusty weapon were caught in his body, but the natural antipathy faeries had to iron should cause his body to try to expel the iron that was battering around inside his body and sickening him. She watched for any sign of the metal and continued to work to keep his fever down.

Still, he stayed that way—thrashing in her bed but unconscious—as night fell.

Finally, a piece of metal worked its way out of his body; it writhed under his skin, and Rika tried not to flinch away as she pushed it toward the still-open wounds and extracted it.

She lit candles and sat beside his bed. At her side were a ceramic bowl, a tiny carved bone knife, a water-filled basin, and the bloodstained wet cloth. In the bowl was the small misshapen piece of metal. If he didn't wake by morning, she'd have to try actively locating the rest of the iron in his body or send for a healer.

"I hate this," she told the unconscious faery.

Still he said nothing.

A second piece of the poisonous metal pressed against his skin as his body tried to expel it. This time, she had to cut into his skin to remove it. He gasped, but he didn't wake.

She stayed by his side, watching for more of the iron pieces. They were so small that once they were removed they didn't hurt him or her unless they actually touched them. Unfortunately, most of them were also inside his body.

By the time he finally opened his eyes, it was midday, and the cavern was illuminated by a blazing fire that cast dancing shadows over the stalactites and stalagmites, and the candles were dripping wax on various surfaces of the room.

Sionnach had dark shadows under his eyes and sallow skin. He looked around the cavern, his gaze taking in every detail before looking back at her. "Where's Jayce?"

Rika knew she shouldn't be surprised: Sionnach had been supportive of her interest in Jayce. That didn't change the absurdity of his question. He'd been stabbed, and his first question was about a mortal boy he barely knew. "Jayce is with his friends; I couldn't bring both of you."

"I'm here. Go get him."

Rika shook her head. "I can't leave you alone and unprotected."

"Rika—"

"No." She grabbed the basin and walked away from him, trying to hide her frustration. "You have *iron* bits in your body. It was rusty and parts shattered inside you."

"You can't leave him where Maili can reach him."

Standing in the middle of the cavern, basin clenched in her hand, she stared at the injured faery. "No. What I can't do is leave *you* here with iron in your skin, Shy. The pieces need to come out. I have two of them, but there are more."

"So?" He shook his head. "Jayce is vulnerable. I need you to be with Jayce."

"You need—" She cut herself off and walked away. Slowly, she poured out the water and then went to the little stream that ran through the cavern. She knelt and scooped up a basin full of fresh water. Convinced that her temper was back in check, she said, "You *need* taking care of. He's staying with friends. Just—"

"He's a mortal."

The water was ice cold, a fact for which she had been grateful earlier when the fever had threatened to burn

Sionnach's skin. She carried it over to him and resumed her seat on the ground. "He's a smart mortal."

Sionnach opened his mouth to object, but instead, he let out a small sound of pain as the skin of his arm started pulsing, like something alive was squirming under it. He blanched as he looked at his arm. "She was clever this time."

"No. She was stupid." Rika tried to keep her now rising temper in check. He had confirmed that it *was* Maili who'd stabbed him. With a calm she didn't quite feel, Rika lifted the tiny bone knife and made a small incision in his arm. Her face emotionless, she plucked the minuscule fleck of rusty metal out and quickly dropped it into the ceramic bowl with the two other tiny pieces of metal already in it.

"Three for luck." She took the bowl away, and after discarding the poison, she retrieved a new but tattered cloth and a bowl of clean water. As she walked back to his side, she said, "You know we can't ignore something like this."

Despite how haggard he looked, Sionnach's smile suddenly became a familiar tricksy one, the expression she'd seen so often and feared she'd never see again. Even sick and on his back, he was spirited, and she couldn't help but smile back at him.

"We?" he repeated. "There's a *we* in this, princess? I thought you were unwilling to get involved in faery politics?"

Carefully not looking at him, she sat on the ground next to the bed where he was recovering, dipped the cloth into the bowl of water, and then squeezed out the excess. His words forced her to face the part of being a faery that she had tried for years to avoid, but in the past few weeks, she'd been drawn into the world of faery politics and conflicts. First, Maili'd struck Jayce, then she'd fought with Rika, and now she'd stabbed Sionnach.

Sionnach didn't speak as she wiped away the fresh blood on his arm with the wet rag in her hand. He watched her motions, but avoided looking into her eyes. She'd had enough conversations with him over the past few years that she knew that he was merely waiting for her to admit what she'd rather not say. This alone she knew with complete certainty when it came to the fox faery: he was wily and patient.

She rinsed the blood from the rag in her hand, looking at the water rather than him, and said, "I don't seem to have many choices right now. The only other faery strong enough to hold order in the desert is bleeding in my bed."

"And, sadly, far too weak for either of us to enjoy my being here . . ."

Her gaze snapped to him, and her cheeks colored with embarrassment. "You shouldn't say things like that."

"Why? It's who I am."

"But it's not . . . we're not . . ." She tried to look stern as she wiped blood from his stomach, looking at her hand rather than at his face. "You just shouldn't say things like that, Sionnach."

"So it's Sionnach now, not Shy?" he murmured.

She met his gaze. "I can't . . . we're not like that."

He looked serious now. He put his hand over hers, keeping her from escaping. "I know. You need a relationship without any ulterior motives. I knew that Jayce could give you that. I can't."

She paused, processing the implications of his words and the feel of his hand on hers. If she were more fey, she'd focus on the offer that he wasn't making, at the admission he wasn't speaking, but she couldn't think about that. Her body tensed as if she were poised to flee. All she said was, "So you have ulterior motives?"

"Always." Sionnach didn't look the least bit apologetic—nor did he remove his hand from hers.

"Will you tell me what they are?"

"Someday." His tricksy smile returned, chasing away the seriousness that felt strangely heavy between them. "Some of them."

"How am I to trust you then?"

Sionnach squeezed her hand once and then entwined his fingers with hers. He pulled her hand away from his bare skin but held on to her, keeping her from retreating. "You aren't to trust me . . . not on everything. Trust your instincts. Trust your judgment."

"You're—"

"A faery by blood," he interrupted. "Just like Keenan."

She wasn't sure what Sionnach was admitting—that he was manipulative, capricious, deceitful?—but she did know that nothing she could think of was particularly comforting. Trusting a faery was what had gotten her into this strange world; it was why she had never had the mortal life that she'd wanted. Despite all of that, she *did* trust Sionnach. He was the closest friend she'd ever had in either her mortal or fey lives.

Sionnach used his grasp on her hand to turn her arm and then kissed the underside of her wrist where her pulse was thudding. "And, like the Summer King, I've never been prone to lingering; that's why I didn't try to get in your bed when we met. Jayce is good for you right now. I'm not. Not in that way. . . ."

Despite having known Sionnach for years, she felt off-kilter. She hadn't felt like a human girl for a very long time, but Sionnach was right in that she didn't want to be cast away as if she were unimportant. At the same time, she felt foolish that she hadn't realized that Sionnach had genuinely looked at her in any way other than as a friend. He'd flirted for years, but he was a fox faery. It was his nature. She'd thought he might have had such thoughts a couple of weeks ago on the night when he wore Jayce's face and pretended he would kiss her—and the next day—but then he'd helped her explain what she was to Jayce.

"You wanted me to be with Jayce," she half protested. It seemed odd that he would admit that he'd thought of her in a way other than friends, yet continue to push her toward Jayce. She wasn't sure what to think, but she was unsettled by the realizations that Sionnach was eliciting—and the way he watched her.

"Go get Jayce, Rika," Sionnach said gently as he released his hold on her hand. "I'm fine for the few moments you'll be away, and you have the mortal boy you wanted."

Rika was silent as she watched him. She ran her recently freed fingers around the top rim of the water bowl. "I care for you, but I love him. He doesn't know, but I fell in love before he knew I existed. I just want that, to be loved—even though loving mortals is foolish."

"Love—even with such finite creatures—is *everything*, Rika," Sionnach said gently. "He's what I want for you, and I'm sure you're worried about him. Just go fetch him. Please?"

"Why?"

Sionnach pushed himself into a sitting position and reached out to take her hand from the bowl she now clutched tightly. She let go of it and instead busied herself putting extra pillows behind him so he was propped up on them.

"*Why?*" she repeated. "Why do you want me to be with Jayce if you . . ." She felt stupid, trying to verbalize what he didn't say.

"There's a price for spilling secrets," he warned her.

"I know what you are, Shy. I've known since we met. 'Fox faeries are equally loyal and deceitful,'" Rika said it as if she was reading it from a page. She shook her head. "I had a lot of time to read when I was hiding out here those first years—and even more *before* . . . when I carried winter. Cursed faeries are solitary faeries. Formerly mortal faeries are even more so."

Sionnach looked like he wanted to say something, but he didn't.

Rika picked up the knife from the floor, buying a moment to hide her hurt expression. She handed the knife to him hilt first. "I've *always* known what and who you were, but I still trusted you. I *do* trust you."

"You probably shouldn't," he said, but he looked happier than he usually did—not secretive, not tricksy, just genuinely happy.

Rika shrugged. "It sounds like I should. You just admitted that you cared enough not to seduce me."

"What I need from you matters more than sex." He gave her an impish grin before adding, "You're awfully scrawny anyhow. I usually like—"

"I know." She held up a hand, grateful that he'd resorted to his usual lighthearted ways. "I've heard enough stories."

Sionnach laughed, and then he promptly put a hand atop his injury. "Ouch . . . I'll stay right here and"—he glanced down at his wounds and scowled—"not laugh while you're gone."

"I could stay," she offered.

"No." He made a shooing gesture. "Go get Jayce. Please?"

"Okay." Rika turned and walked away, but she paused at the doorway and said, "I'll be back as fast as I can."

When Rika reached the skate park, she stopped and remained invisible briefly, standing behind the mortals who were gathered there. She felt a strange mix of inclusion and exclusion around Jayce's friends. On the other side of a wire-mesh fence—coated steel far too toxic for a faery to touch—Jayce sat with Del on metal bleachers while Kayley was on a vertical half-pipe. The boys watched her. Del's skateboard was propped next to him, but neither of the boys took it out to the ramps. Kayley was the artist here.

Jayce grinned at Del as Kayley executed another nice trick. Several other people noticed her prowess as well. "Your girl would shame me if I went out there," Jayce said.

Del preened. "She shames *me*. I swear I'm going to get as good as her, but she comes out harder every time."

They watched her for a moment, and Rika was struck at how different they were from the men she'd known in her human life—and the faeries she knew in the courts. Keenan had believed that women were to be delicate, that men were to be better at every act of skill. Rika had tried to be that, even after she was fey. It hadn't worked. She smiled to herself at the thought of Donia, the girl who'd become Winter Queen. *She* wasn't ever meek, and from the rumors that had made their way to the desert so far, neither was the Summer Queen. Not for the first time, Rika hoped that both formerly mortal faeries were making Keenan squirm.

On the other side of the chain fence, Del and Jayce continued to discuss Kayley. "She outskates me, but on a climb"—Del grinned at Jayce—"I get her back."

After a few more minutes, Kayley walked up to the guys.

"Nice." Jayce gestured with his chin toward the ramp where Kayley had been.

Although she shrugged like she was unconcerned, her posture and the grin on her face revealed her pleasure as she accepted the compliment Jayce offered her.

"I've seen worse." Del extended his bottle of water to Kayley.

"Yeah, you." Kayley drained the rest of the bottle and

tossed it into a recycling bin. She smiled at Del, who promptly caught her by the hips and pulled her toward him.

"Compared to you?" He paused and kissed her lightly. "Every day."

"Get off your ass then." Kayley looked from Del to Jayce. "Neither of you are going to get any better if all you do is sit around watching me."

At that, Rika decided it was time to interrupt. If Jayce went to the ramps, she'd be left in the awkward position of trying to explain why she couldn't come inside the park and why she couldn't stay. She backed farther away from the park, and then after a quick glance around to verify that no one was looking in her direction, she became visible to human eyes. Jayce and Del wouldn't notice her for a few moments, so she waited, walking slowly toward them. She couldn't approach the metal bleachers and the fence surrounding the park, but she wouldn't have to. They'd see her, or she'd call out.

After a few steps, Kayley noticed her and waved. Del glanced over his shoulder, waved, and then grabbed his board. They both said, "Later, Jayce."

Rika waited, knowing that Jayce would come to her so she didn't have to come any closer to the poisonous metal. She felt her cheeks flush as he smiled at her, and she couldn't believe that he was hers now, that he saw her and wanted to be with her.

"Everyone okay?" Jayce asked as he reached her side.

She nodded, and he pulled her into his arms. Before the last few weeks, Rika had only been kissed a few times in her life, chaste kisses that didn't leave her feeling consumed, but in the past couple of weeks, she'd discovered why people kissed. As Jayce's lips pressed against hers, his arms tightened around her. Even still, she felt like they were too far apart, and when he pulled away, she wanted to whimper at the loss. Instead, she asked, "Come with me?"

She entwined their hands, unable to be this close to him without touching.

"Anywhere," Jayce agreed.

This was what she'd wanted, this togetherness, this hunger to be with another person. She'd thought she'd lost the chance at it when she'd believed Keenan's lies, and now, she couldn't imagine life without it. Someday, this would pass. Unless they were cursed, mortals didn't become faeries, so Jayce would leave her someday. Rika hadn't told him that, not wanting to bring up how fleeting their time was. For now, she had found the heady mix of *like* and *want* that she'd been dreaming of for years.

She smiled, and they started across the desert . . . fading to invisible as they walked away from the people in town. Things might be unstable in the desert, and she had no doubt that there would be conflict until Maili realized that she couldn't become Alpha. Right now, though, Sionnach was alive and healing, and Jayce was at Rika's side. Both her faery friend and her mortal boyfriend were safe, and Rika couldn't stop the smile that came over her.

CHAPTER 12

Sionnach knew that the Summer King was standing nearby: Keenan didn't exactly try to hide the heat that radiated from his body. No one else, save for the newly ascended Summer Queen, would exude such heat, and there was no reason that the new queen would visit the home of a former Winter Girl. So without opening his eyes, Sionnach knew that the Summer King stood in the mouth of the room in Rika's cave where Sionnach was reclining, half-propped on the mound of pillows Rika had arranged behind him.

When he *did* open his eyes, Sionnach had to resist the urge to grin. The wide-eyed shock on the Summer King's face was enough to improve even the lowest of moods, and his temper was accompanied by eddies of heat that made the air shimmer.

"What are *you* doing *there*?" Keenan didn't gesture, but the disdain and possessiveness were both clear in his tone. Even now, the Summer King did not expect to see someone else in the bed of one of his former pseudo-beloveds.

Sionnach offered his practiced expression of wide-eyed innocence and said, "Recovering."

The bowl with the hilt of the knife in it was hidden on the opposite side of Sionnach's body, so Keenan wouldn't see it. To keep the Summer King's temper pricked and his attention diverted, Sionnach smiled in the way of the falsely modest and added, "Forgive me for not standing, but I can't find the energy just yet."

The answering heat flare was enough to raise the temperature in the cave, enough to explain the fine sheen of sweat on Sionnach's body. It wasn't comfortable, but it was useful at hiding the truth. He waited as Keenan's gaze took in the candles, the glasses beside the bed, and the fact that Sionnach was seemingly naked. There were moments in every faery's life that were too perfect to have been planned, and Sionnach was having just such a moment as he reclined in Rika's bed grinning while the faery who had caused such upheaval in Rika's life—*and* in their desert—very obviously misinterpreted the clues.

"Were you looking for something?" Sionnach queried. In a moment of feigned modesty, he pulled the blanket higher as if to cover his upper chest, intentionally drawing the Summer King's eye to his bared arms and shoulders. In shifting the blanket, one of Sionnach's legs became partially exposed. The result, as Sionnach intended, was that he appeared to be sans trousers too.

After a disgusted look at Sionnach, Keenan asked, "Where is she?"

"Rika?" Sionnach stretched and, trying not to wince, rolled onto his hip. "She's out."

"I need to talk to her."

"Hmmm. I don't think she's interested." Casually, Sionnach reached down and lifted one of the glasses Rika had left next to him. He took a sip, stalling to hide his fight with pain, and watched Keenan. Then, he swallowed and said, "You had your chance. She's moved on to better things."

"I'm not here for that. I respect Rika—"

Sionnach couldn't help the bark of laughter that escaped his lips. "*Sure* you do." He dragged out the words. "*I* respect Rika; you upset her. You hurt her. I've been looking out for her while you were busy ruining other mortals' lives."

"I want to talk to her. We have business—"

"Let me guess. Fealty? The benefit of your court's protection in exchange for meddling with our lives?" Sionnach sat up, holding the sheet to his abdomen, casually keeping it over his wounds as if he were protecting his modesty. "Where were you all these years when we struggled to keep *any* semblance of order in the desert? Where were you with your offers when I was getting bloodied to keep the unruly ones from slaughtering mortals? Not interested."

"I'm not asking you. I'm here for Rika." Sun sparks glittered around Keenan as he became increasingly agitated.

Sionnach looked to the hallway behind Keenan. Rika's silhouette was barely visible in the dark. This opportunity was too good to ignore. King or not, the arrogant court faery needed to be reminded that there were things that were not acceptable, like leaving Rika so sorrowful that she had hidden herself away from everyone for years. Although Sionnach had hidden his own sorrow at seeing her so lost and confused, he certainly hadn't forgotten it. He never would. To Keenan, Rika was one of scores of mortals whose lives had been changed irreparably by nothing more than the bad luck of his having noticed them. For nine hundred years, the Summer King had wooed mortal after mortal, trying to convince them to love him, hoping that they would love him enough to take the ridiculous test to determine if they were the one mortal who could free him. Those who loved him enough were the unluckiest: for their foolish trust in him, they were cursed to carry ice in their bodies until the next girl agreed to the test. If Sionnach had been a different faery, if he'd been Keenan's friend, he would feel sorry for the king's centuries of searching. He wasn't, though. He was Rika's friend.

He stared at Keenan, offering him his most convincingly innocent expression. "It won't matter what you're here to say. Rika doesn't follow very well; she's more of a leader."

"Rika?" Keenan gave Sionnach a look of incredulity at that. "She was a sweet girl when I met her. Time doesn't change that. She might have a few fits of temper, but—"

"But what?" Rika interrupted as she walked closer to them.

Keenan turned to face her. He shrugged, arrogant and apparently not concerned that she'd heard his idiocy. "I came back to give you another chance to discuss this. I can give you the security I never could before. You could keep order here in the desert for me. You give me your vow, and I give you my strength to get things safer here. It's better for everyone. . . ."

Sionnach laughed, interrupting the Summer King, who fixed him with a glare. Sionnach's laughter was only a little forced. Logic had begun reminding him that he shouldn't use those stomach muscles, that moving and laughing were liable to make him cry in pain before long. He swallowed against the sound that wanted to crawl out of his throat.

"Shy, no laughing," Rika ordered, and he knew that she was well aware of the way it was making him feel.

"Yes, Rika," he demurred, giving her a very obedient look, and then he smirked at Keenan. "She's a natural *leader*, only a fool wouldn't see that."

Keenan continued to glare at Sionnach, holding the other faery's eyes for a heartbeat or two, and then returned his attention to Rika. "We can talk out the details. Things are different now. You'd be an extension of my court. It's not a difficult task, and you could enlist whatever"—he gestured vaguely at Sionnach—"faeries you wanted as staff."

"Did you miss the part where I said *no* when you were here before?" Resolutely, Rika walked past Keenan and came to gently sit down on the bed beside Sionnach, putting herself between them. Her hand brushed his cheek gently, a gesture that looked like affection but Sionnach knew to be a subtle way of checking his fever.

As she withdrew her hand, Sionnach realized that he was barely resisting touching her. He'd let Keenan think that she was his. She wasn't. He'd known that for decades. They were friends. He'd all but shoved Jayce into her arms. Still . . . he could rationalize it away right now as simply encouraging the image he had set before the Summer King. He ran his fingertips over Rika's upper arm, enjoying touching her as he so rarely could. She didn't pull away.

"I'm not interested in what you are offering," Rika told Keenan, her voice soft but firm. Her body was motionless, but Sionnach felt the tension in her muscles. He didn't know if it was her anger or his touch that made her so stiff. Just in case his touch was making her unhappy, Sionnach stilled his hand.

"I don't want to hear anything you have to say," Rika said.

Keenan raked his hand through his hair. "Be reasonable, Rika. You can't think that having this many uncontrolled faeries without leadership is *wise*. The Summer Court can establish order here. If you help—"

"No." She glanced over her shoulder at Sionnach then and added, "I have all the help I need."

Sionnach reclined, letting himself relax farther into the pillows now that she was there. The pain from hiding his injury and moving as if he were unharmed had made him feel sick. A wise Alpha didn't show such things—especially to court faeries who were determined to take over where they weren't wanted. Moreover, an Alpha didn't show weakness to the one who'd hurt the faery he most wanted to shelter. Sionnach wrapped an arm around Rika's waist and closed his eyes as if he were bored. "Wake me when he's gone."

"He's leaving *now.*" Rika wrapped her hand around Sionnach's where it rested on her, keeping him held tightly to her, letting him know that his embrace was wanted. This, at least, was familiar territory with them. He had embraced her a few times over the decades when she was upset—usually because of the Summer King's unwanted visits.

Sionnach could feel her tremble as he held her. Seeing Keenan had always upset her, and the helplessness Sionnach felt every time hadn't faded. He couldn't undo the hurt, the self-doubt, the sorrow that Keenan's actions had caused her. He couldn't even strike out at the faery king. All he could do was stay by her side, and try to help her when he had a chance. He squeezed her hand reassuringly, reminding her that she was not alone.

"There are other faeries who would be strong enough to run the desert for me if you won't, Rika." Keenan's words were spoken softly, but the threat in them was implicit: he would control the desert with or without her.

Sionnach's eyes snapped open as his temper flared, but even the strongest Alpha was no match for a faery king. Years ago, when Keenan was a bound king, Sionnach might have considered attacking him. He would've lost, but he might have survived it. Now, though? The Summer King was unbound; he was all but invincible. A fight would likely end in death, or at the least, such a severe defeat that Sionnach would be useless to Rika. And attempting anything while he had poison in his body would be a potentially fatal act.

Rika, however, didn't seem to have even reacted to Keenan's quiet threat. She said only, "You need to go, Keenan. I don't have anything more to say to you, and I don't want to see you."

The Summer King, however, was nothing if not persistent. He was a faery who had spent nine centuries seeking one girl. He didn't surrender easily. "Think about what's best," he said. "The solitaries here don't need to be without protection. The Summer Court has a plan to create subregions with local rulers and—"

"No," she cut him off. "We are strong enough without you. No one bothers us out here."

"But if there's trouble from one of the other courts—"

"Why would they bring their conflicts here? Our only troubles are from our own, and Shy and I are strong enough to mete out discipline. You made me stronger than most every faery when you stole my humanity. I didn't need your help these past years." She faltered then, looking bereft for a moment.

"You were already strong inside. That's why he chose you," Sionnach murmured gently, giving her the encouragement she deserved. "Still are. You can hold order over the desert, Rika. Without him. Without me."

Rika glanced back at Sionnach. An all-too-familiar look of worry crossed her face. "Am I? You were always Alpha here."

"Only because the stronger faery didn't take it from me. You're strong and brave and smart," Sionnach told her honestly, not caring that they had an audience. "You *know* that. We don't need him here."

After a grateful smile at him, Rika looked back at Keenan and announced, "We have nothing to discuss."

As Keenan glared at Sionnach, heat wafted toward them. The Summer King said bluntly, "Maili has approached me."

"Rule of might, sweetheart." Sionnach gestured in the air with one arm, pointing toward Keenan. He smiled sweetly and added, "Maili can't act as liaison unless she's the Alpha, the top. She's not. Rika's the strongest faery here. Aren't you, princess?"

"I am." She nodded her head and straightened her shoulders. "This is solitary territory, not court territory. You have no rights unless the Alpha allows it . . . and since Shy and I are the strongest faeries here, and I'm telling you *again* that you are not welcome here, you need to go away."

Sionnach made an agreeing murmur, once more trying to seem unconcerned that Keenan was there, but inside he was rejoicing. Rika was acting as if she was already Alpha, as if she was the one in power here. *This* was what he'd been trying to convince Rika to notice for years: she was strong. She could rule the desert. It was unfortunate that it took him getting stabbed and taunting the Summer King to get her near the point of accepting the truth, but that mattered little in the big scheme of things. Rika was declaring herself.

"Leave, Keenan," Rika demanded.

"Good idea, princess. Make the distraction go away." Sionnach released Rika's hand.

Rika's voice sounded like laughter was about to replace words as she told Keenan, "It's past time for you to go, Keenan."

Then, she stood, walked over and took Keenan's arm, and led him to the mouth of the cave. "Go. And don't walk into my home again without my permission. You have no authority over me—or right to walk into my sleeping chamber."

"Ashamed of your choices?" Keenan asked.

After a quiet moment, Rika answered, "Only the one, but that was a long time ago."

Chapter 13

Keenan stared at the faery he'd once hoped would be his queen. "You're ashamed of loving me?"

Rika laughed. It was painfully different from the soft sound that he'd once found so enchanting. When she was a mortal, she was sweet. She'd trusted him, looked at him with such hope in her eyes, smiled at him with love. He still remembered her that way. He remembered all of the formerly mortal girls he'd wooed. Most of all, though, he remembered those rare girls who had been brave enough or in love enough to take the test to be his queen. Until this year, they'd all failed, but they were special. *Rika* was special.

"I'm not ashamed of it," he said quietly. "You were br—"

"No," she interrupted. "I don't want to hear your flattery, Keenan."

He stood silently beside her for a moment before muttering, "The fox doesn't deserve you."

"Sionnach knows me better than you ever did." She shook her head. "All those years I was cursed to stand against you, I'm not sure you ever tried to know me."

There were words he could say, wicked phrases and lovely reminders, but they would only hide the lie. He hadn't known her. Sometimes, he thought that the only faeries he truly knew were the Winter Queens—the one he loved and the one he'd killed. For nine hundred years, he'd spent all of his time seeking his missing Summer Queen and trying to rule without his full power. He was realizing of late that he had made more than a few mistakes.

"Knowing you doesn't mean deserving you" was all he said.

Rika stared at him for a moment, and foolishly, he felt a brush of hope that they could talk rationally. Unfortunately, that hope faded as she folded her arms over her chest and said, "Go away. Don't come back here."

He couldn't truly blame her for thinking she could confront a *regent* so boldly. It had been her role from the time she became fey until Donia became the next Winter Girl. He lifted a hand to brush back her hair, but she moved out of his reach. "You can't demand that, not of me," he told her. "Not now."

Instead of replying, she turned and returned to her cave. Later, he could try again, but for now, he let her go. Some battles were about steadily wearing away at the defenses, not winning in one glorious fight. He wasn't done here.

Nonetheless, Keenan felt the weight of failure on his

shoulders as he left Rika's cave. The desert had always been one of his solaces; it was one of the rare places in the world where the last Winter Queen had been unable to extend her power. When Rika had first been freed from the then–Winter Queen's curse and fled to the Mojave Desert, Keenan had believed that he'd have a future ally there. She'd been angry during her time as a Winter Girl, good at convincing girls not to trust him, but she'd loved him once. He'd believed that her anger would fade, that the core of her love was still there. Now, as he walked across the scorching ground, he realized he'd been tragically wrong. Like both his Summer Queen and the new Winter Queen, Rika simply didn't *trust* him.

There were times when he wished that he could explain, could make them understand that he was as trapped by the curse as they had been. The problem, of course, was that they were trapped because of *his* choices, whereas he was trapped because of the choices of the last Winter Queen. She'd bound his powers, hidden them away inside a mortal girl so he couldn't stand against Winter, and he was left seeking a single grain of sand in the expanse of a great desert. Literally, billions of girls could have been the one he needed. Each time he chose a girl, she was cursed; her humanity faded. She became either a Summer Girl, whose very life required contact with him, or the Winter Girl, who was filled with ice. He understood the anger some of them felt, probably *deserved* it, but if he hadn't tried, the earth would freeze. Over time, every mortal and every faery not of the Winter Court would die.

He bowed his head as he walked. There hadn't been a lot of choices left to him. He'd had to try to find his missing queen. He'd succeeded after nine hundred years, but somehow even success came with problems. His queen refused his affections; the faery he loved had become the new Winter Queen; and war seemed imminent. Even after completing a seemingly impossible challenge, he was still losing.

As Keenan reached a rocky outcropping, the faery he'd been contacted by stepped out.

"Your, ah, highness, or . . . what do you call a king?" Maili asked.

Her attitude irritated him, so he ignored the question. "What do you need?"

"You weren't able to reason with Rika. I can do it. I'll defeat her for you."

Keenan looked at the faery. Her tone was far more impertinent than he was accustomed to these days, and her posture was anything but respectful. He didn't expect meekness, but whether he was her king or not, he was a regent. He was the embodiment of summer itself, protector and leader of a court. That deserved a bit of respect.

Honestly, he simply didn't understand the solitaries; something about their lack of court always unsettled him. Court, especially the Summer Court, wasn't just about order. They reveled. They danced. They cared for the other members of their court. Sure, there were questions of obedience, but he didn't ask his faeries to do anything that wasn't for their own good or the good of the court. He had spent his entire life striving to make them safe, to protect them from the cold that had threatened, to lead them even though he'd been weakened by the curse. Choosing to be solitary wasn't something he could fathom.

"No," he said. "Talk to her first."

Maili flinched as if he'd struck her. "*Talk* to her?"

For a moment Keenan thought about the angry way Rika and her fox had looked at him. They'd never believe he was trying to be fair, never believe he was trying to do the right thing. They saw only their own desire to keep the desert, not the fact that he could now protect them. The desert was a place of heat; it was only logical that it should become part of his territory. Admittedly, his interests weren't totally selfless. He *was* a faery. Allies were increasingly necessary to his court right now. Skirmishes seemed imminent. The Dark King was angry, and the Winter Queen was upset about the time he'd been spending with his queen. Even his own court held the possibility of conflict as his Summer Queen discovered how much he'd misled her in his attempts to hide her mortal lover's whereabouts. Trouble was definitely coming from at *least* one side.

When the Summer Queen's mortal had returned from Faerie, changed into a faery for half the year, Keenan had realized he'd lost the battle for her affections. He could keep fighting, and maybe he would. Right now, he felt a bit like retreating and licking his wounds. He'd lost his advisor to the Dark Court, his beloved to the Winter Court, and his destined queen to a mortal *boy*. He wasn't going to completely give up. He was the Summer King, but he had retreated to seek allies—not just to strengthen his court but also because it would feel good to have a victory.

But I failed at this too.

With an expression that wouldn't reveal the morass of emotions inside him, he stared at Maili and repeated, "Talk to Rika."

At that, Keenan walked past her. The desert wasn't the only place where he could find allies. As he'd searched for his queen for centuries, he'd met a lot of solitaries, many of whom were organized into loose groups like those here in the desert. He'd done what he could here. Maili would talk to Rika, and then Keenan would follow up. With that in mind, he left the desert behind and headed toward the forests of California. Out there they had the tall redwoods and the wide sequoias. In the boughs of those trees and in the shadows of those forests, faeries made their homes. Perhaps some among them would be willing to join his court now that he was unbound.

Chapter 14

From the room where Jayce was waiting, he could see into the central opening of Rika's cave. Through a fissure in the wall, he'd watched the glowing faery, the one Rika and Sionnach had called Keenan, leave. Jayce hadn't heard every word, but he'd heard enough to know that this faery thought he had a right to Rika's attention—and that Sionnach was acting like Rika was his. Despite everything that had happened the past couple of weeks since he had met Rika, Jayce still knew people. Faeries might have been a big surprise to him, but he'd come to understand pretty quickly that for all their differences, they still had the sort of emotions humans had. It didn't take a genius to notice that Sionnach had feelings for Rika. She, however, acted like she was oblivious. Jayce didn't know if that was because she was trying not to hurt Sionnach or because she had decided she didn't date faeries. Either way, the emotions weren't as hidden as either faery seemed to think.

What am I doing with her?

Jayce walked to the mouth of the cave where Rika stood. He wanted to wrap his arms around her, although he suspected that the smart thing to do was to leave. Rika didn't look at him. Instead, she stood staring out across the desert. He wasn't sure what secrets she hid, but he knew that the past was something she avoided discussing. As Jayce looked at the shadowy desert vista, he could see light radiating from Keenan as he strode across the desert like a ground-level meteor.

"How many faeries are in line for your attention?" Jayce forced himself to stand slightly to the side and behind her.

Rika glanced back and frowned at him. "None, why?"

"The one who left sounded—"

"Keenan's a jerk," Rika interrupted. Her tone and expression softened instantly as she looked at Jayce. She stayed like that, silently watching him for several heartbeats.

"What?" He didn't soften; he couldn't. He was only eighteen, not looking for a wife or anything, but he wanted a girlfriend. He wanted *this girl* in his life with a ferocity that had shocked him.

For the first time since the night they'd first kissed here in this same cave, he could tell that Rika had just decided to reveal more about herself. Her expression tensed, fear and nervousness filling her eyes, and then she relaxed visibly. "He was the one who made me this."

"He made you a faery?"

"A long time ago. He thought I could be someone he

needed. I tried. I failed. This"—she gestured at herself and the barren cave around her—"is part of the price. The worst part was that there were full decades when my body was filled with ice."

Suddenly, she seemed vulnerable and very, very sad, and Jayce regretted pushing her to tell him about her life. "Rika . . ."

"It's okay," she assured him. "I'm trying to be open about everything like you asked, but it's not easy to talk about it."

"I'm sorry." He pulled her into his arms and held her in silence.

She didn't cry, but she did curl into his embrace, accepting his comfort or maybe forgiving him for wanting to know. He felt a flash of guilt at the thought. He'd dated a few girls, but he wasn't sure how to truly date Rika. Part of dating was getting to know each other, but it was hard to do that when the girl in question was some sort of supernatural creature with secrets too big for him to truly grasp.

Moments of silence passed, and he wished he had a clue how to be in her world without asking for answers that she wasn't willing to share. He didn't want her to be unhappy, but he wanted to know her. He stroked her hair and kept her clasped tightly to his chest. Talking wasn't the right way to grow closer to her right now. After a moment, though, he had to ask, "How's Sionnach?"

He knew that the faery was obviously alive and alert; Jayce had heard his voice. That didn't mean he was fine, however.

"Weak." Rika pulled back a little and looked toward the tunnel leading to the cavern where Sionnach was resting. "He'll be fine in time, but she poisoned him. He's not going to be truly well anytime soon."

Jayce nodded, trying to find the right words to tell her that he was there for her without asking any questions that would make her grow quieter.

But then Rika blurted, "There's no one but *you* in my life."

When he looked at her, she took a deep, shuddering breath and continued shakily, "I've been alone for . . . ever, really. Keenan left me when he realized I wasn't who he hoped I was. Shy's been my friend, but we're not . . . we've never . . . been anything else."

"He's something to you." Jayce wasn't accusing, merely stating the obvious. He wasn't the sort of guy to make a scene or be possessive, but he wasn't going to pretend he didn't notice what was right in front of him either.

"Not what you are." She blushed. "I've never felt like I do with you."

Jayce paused before he said, "He's in your life in ways I'm not."

"And you're here in ways he isn't." She looked back out to the now darkened and shadowy desert. He knew without her saying it that she'd been checking to make sure that Keenan had left. Now that the glowing faery was gone, Jayce could see her visibly relax. Quietly, she said, "I can't change who I am. I won't. I made that mistake once."

Jayce stepped behind her and pulled her against him. His arms wrapped around her, and he rested his cheek against her head. "I don't want you to change. I just want to *know* you. Everything seems like such a secret."

He could feel Rika tense in his arms, but he didn't let go of her.

"I want to be with you," he added. "Just talk to me, please?"

She leaned back into Jayce's arms. "Shy sent me to see you today. He stayed here, injured, while I came to you. He's my *friend*. Until you, he's been my only true friend."

Jayce kissed her head. "And the other one? Keenan?"

Rika laughed bitterly. "He's never been my friend. He's never been my lover either." She turned in Jayce's arms, so she was facing him. "You can trust me, Jayce. There's no competition for my heart. My attention sometimes . . . but not my heart. Until you, I'd never even been properly kissed. No one wanted to draw with me or hike in the desert. I watched you, wanting you, and now I have you in my arms. I want to be with *you*."

Jayce leaned down and kissed her, meaning to be sweet, worrying that he'd been too forward after what she just admitted. He believed what she'd just said was true, too, because according to Rika faeries couldn't lie. It seemed crazy that the beautiful girl in his arms had been alone for most of her life. It was a little scary.

And cool, he admitted to himself.

"I didn't know you were so innocent. I won't push you."

He started to step away from her, but she held him close and kissed him thoroughly. One of her hands entwined in his dreads, clutching them to hold him to her.

When they parted, she whispered, "You're not pushing. I'm trying to let you in, but I've been on my own for longer than the town even existed. It takes time. Ask me something else."

Jayce held her tightly, one hand on her back, one hand cradling her head. He wasn't sure how he'd gotten so lucky. Rika was unlike anyone he'd ever met, and she wanted to be with *him*. They'd figure it out.

They stayed like that for a few moments, enjoying the closeness that they were creating. When he let go, he took Rika's hand and asked, "So why was Keenan here? If he doesn't want to date you. . . . Did he want to try to be friends?"

"No." Rika made a sound that might've been a laugh. "He wants me to be his *subject*, swear loyalty to him. In exchange, he'll back me in controlling the desert."

"So you'd be like . . . a sheriff or something? In charge of them?" Jayce sat on the ledge.

Rika sat next to him. "Yeah, but I don't need *him* to be in charge. Might and will determine power out here. Shy was the one who held order. He's Alpha, first in the faeries who choose to live here. To change the rules means changing the Alpha. Most of the rules are so minor that no one bothers. With a king though"—she scowled—"he'd have a host of rules. We're not children to be controlled."

"But with Shy injured . . . who's that make Alpha?"

"Me," she said it softly, glancing at him from behind a bit of hair that had fallen into her face. "It means that I need to be ready to deal with a few challenges—unless I have someone strong supporting me."

"Like Keenan."

She nodded. "But Keenan's support comes with costs I won't pay."

Jayce frowned. "Like?"

"Obedience. I've been on my own for forever though. Even as Winter Girl, I had no ruler. I was between two courts, caught in their game, but not sworn to either." Rika looked fierce, and Jayce was suddenly reminded of wild animals. She might have begun her life as a mortal, but there was something majestic about her that was more than human.

"So tell him no."

"I did." She lifted her chin a little. "It felt good too. Now I just need to hold things together until Shy is well; then he can deal with a couple dozen moody faeries. Remind them who's in charge."

"But you're stronger? Why was he in charge then?"

She shrugged. "Shy's strong, and I didn't want to be involved. He was here when I got here. . . . I just wanted to draw and be alone." She stood suddenly and reached down for Jayce's hand. "*Now*, I just want to draw and be alone with you."

Smiling, she led him through the tunnel to reach the room where Sionnach was.

The injured faery lifted his head from the bed and looked

at them as they came into the room. He appeared relieved to see them, but he also looked feverish. Sweat was visible on his face and arms. Fresh blood was soaking through the sheet over his stomach. He quickly covered it with his arm and asked, "Keenan's gone?"

"Yes," Jayce confirmed. Quietly, to Rika, he pointed out, "He's bleeding."

"You hurt yourself moving, didn't you?" Rika snapped at him as she went over to check his wounds. She tried to lift his arm, but the injured faery didn't cooperate. "That's what the blanket was hiding."

"Stop!" Sionnach caught her hand in his. He kept the other arm tight to his stomach, holding the sheet in place. He seemed embarrassed. "Jayce? A little help?"

Jayce shook his head. He wasn't going to agree to let anyone stay hurt, especially the faery who was supposed to be keeping order in the desert. "You're injured. Let her look."

Rika scowled at Sionnach and walked away to get more water. "I didn't realize . . . when I walked out—"

Sionnach interjected, "And neither did Keenan."

Rika returned with the basin of water. She dipped a cloth into the basin and then twisted the cloth, squeezing out the excess water. "Who cares what he—"

"Being Alpha means appearing strong even when you aren't."

"Maili." Rika slapped his arm lightly, gesturing for him to move it out of her way, and then scowled when he didn't comply. "She contacted him to let him know you were injured."

"I'm sure she contacted him, but I don't think he knew I was injured." With a sigh, Sionnach moved his arm, letting her pull the sheet away from the bleeding wound on his stomach. "I'm glad he doesn't know I'm this weak."

"Why?" Jayce walked over to a basketlike chair that he'd helped her bring up to the cave last week. It hung from a bent wooden frame. He settled into it, glad that he didn't have to sit on the ground now that there was a comfortable chair. He'd felt awkward sitting on piles of blankets and furs.

Sionnach and Rika both stared at him as he started to swing in the chair. Rika's hand paused midway between the basin and Sionnach's bare stomach, and Sionnach turned a very appraising gaze on Jayce.

"What will happen if Keenan knows?" Jayce opened his bag. "Explain. It's the only way I learn anything, and maybe talking it out will help you make sense of it all."

"Rika is hesitant to be in charge," Sionnach said. "I'm half-useless. Keenan's the king of Summer. Court fey are treacherous, but they're smart. If he thinks we're not strong enough to hold some sort of order here, he'll send out someone with loyalty to him—or openly support Maili."

"Why?" Jayce pulled out a sketch pad.

"Because it's what he does—rally the forces, bring solitaries into his fold, expand his power base." Sionnach grabbed the cloth Rika was now trying to use to wipe his face and gave her a put-upon look. "I can do it myself."

Rika huffed at him in irritation and walked over to get another bowl of the icy water. As she did so, she asked,

"Why is Keenan so interested in *our* home?"

"Because he thinks we should be his because of the heat here?" Sionnach shrugged awkwardly, even now trying to appear uninjured but failing to look convincing. "He always thought we should have been loyal to him."

"So, it could be a revenge thing? Break us to his will now that he's strong. . . ." Rika shook her head. "That doesn't work. Not for Keenan."

Jayce set his sketch pad in his lap for a moment and reached down to pull a thicker pencil from his bag. As he turned the pages, flipping past the rough sketches of Rika—looking fierce, looking vulnerable, looking pensive—he had to remind himself to focus on the conversation. Even as he wanted to know more, he knew he could quickly forget his questions once he began drawing. He looked purposefully at them and again asked, "Why?"

Sionnach wiped the blood from his skin with the rag he hadn't surrendered to Rika, and then pressed the cloth to his wound, wincing as he did so. "I don't like the Summer King, so I hate to say anything *kind* . . . but Rika's right: he's not that petty."

"Strategy." Rika returned to Sionnach's side with a bandage. "There's a benefit to claiming us. If he can bring those of us who are sworn free under his thumb somehow, it increases his strength. It makes him look clever." She scowled at Sionnach and informed him, "I'm wrapping that."

Jayce quickly stifled his burst of laughter, but the quirk

of Sionnach's lips and the way his gaze darted to Jayce made it obvious he'd heard.

"Plus, there are fighters aplenty out here," Sionnach said. "Maybe our little Summer King is thinking of wars to come." He kept his hand pressed to the wound as if Rika hadn't just informed him that she was tending the wound.

"Shy," Rika began warningly.

"Fine." Sionnach tossed the cloth into the washbasin. Carefully, he rolled to his side so she could wrap the bandage round him. The look on his face made it abundantly clear that he wasn't pleased that she was forcing him to be tended. Jayce suspected that Sionnach would be less irritated if not for his presence. This was the faery who was supposed to be the strongest in the desert, and here he was being coddled in front of someone. Jayce looked studiously at his sketch pad while Rika wrapped the bandage around the injured faery. He could see her out of the corner of his eye, but he didn't look up until after she had taken a new sheet and covered Sionnach with it.

"We won't fight his battles for him," Rika said as she stepped away from the now-bandaged faery. "We don't do anything without choice."

"We will if he has an Alpha out here who swears to him." The temper in Sionnach's voice was matched by the fury in his expression, and Jayce began to understand that the intense, changeable moods that Rika sometimes exhibited were simply the way of faeries. Sionnach looked livid where he'd been calm only moments before.

When Rika didn't reply, Sionnach added, "I won't stay here sworn to him, Rika. I won't. You shouldn't either. He's not someone we can trust."

"So is there someone you can trust?" Jayce turned the page and began sketching. It was a way to force himself not to stare at the two faeries, not to remind them that they were letting him see their world so much more than he'd expected.

"Donia!" Rika breathed the word. "She's the new Winter Queen. She exists to oppose him, and she was like me, carrying Winter because we trusted him . . . and were mistreated by him. Her mortality was stolen by him."

"It doesn't matter," Sionnach insisted. "There's always a price with the court fey."

"Donia was once like me, Shy. She's not like them. Maybe—"

"No," he interrupted. "I won't swear to *either* of them—or any other court. We don't need them here. Be my co-Alpha, Rika. Help me through this. Then, I'll get well, and together we'll keep the desert free. If you share Alpha status, we're untouchable."

"Not to a king or queen. He held his throne even when he was a bound king." Rika's voice had grown louder. Suddenly, she let out an audible sigh and walked over to Jayce. She looked down at his sketchbook. "Nice."

Jayce flipped it around to show Sionnach a sketch of himself, but he looked healthy in it, reclining on the bed like a decadent monarch with platters of fruits and a decanter of wine in his reach. The food was overflowing, as if from a horn of plenty.

Sionnach laughed, his anger of a moment ago seemingly vanished, and he asked, "Is that a hint that it's dinnertime?"

"It didn't start that way, but maybe."

Rika shook her head. "You"—she pointed at Sionnach—"rest. I'll be back. . . ."

Sionnach made a faux-serious face. "Yes, Rika."

After she left, Sionnach looked at Jayce and said, "I'm not interested in competing for Rika. She's dating you, and sharing Alpha is *not* romantic."

For a brief moment, Jayce considered pointing out that he knew that Sionnach had romantic feelings for Rika, but he also realized that since faeries didn't lie, Sionnach truly wasn't intending on trying to woo Rika away. Jayce didn't understand how the faery could have such obviously strong feelings for her, but not act on them. He also knew that Sionnach wouldn't tell him, so he simply prompted, "So . . ."

"So help me keep her safe." Sionnach darted a look at the doorway. "Maili is trouble. Rika's been in her cave so long . . . she's never really lived around faeries. She's been near us, but I didn't let anyone bother her. If she's in the world with us, she'll need your love even more. You'll remind her why keeping peace matters."

Jayce didn't respond, but he had a growing suspicion that Sionnach was more involved in Jayce and Rika's relationship than Jayce had realized. That suspicion was confirmed when Sionnach muttered, "I didn't mean for things to happen like this when I finally got you two together."

"*You* got us together?" Jayce gave the faery a stern look, although he was probably about as intimidating as a tortoise was if it were glaring at a coyote. "What did you mean to have happen?"

The fox faery flashed his teeth at Jayce in an approximation of a smile, but he didn't admit anything further.

"Jayce? I have fruit, bread, cheese, but"—she stepped in the doorway and paused, her expression uncomfortable—"*I* can't give you food."

"Right. Faery rules: no food from your hand." Jayce scrambled to his feet. "Sorry."

Sionnach was silent as Jayce followed Rika to her pantry.

After they were out of his earshot, Jayce asked Rika, "So you talked to Sionnach about me before we met?"

She paused. "How did you . . . ?"

"Something Sionnach said," Jayce replied. He started heaping food onto the wooden plate that Rika pointed out. "Does he spend a lot of time around humans?"

"Some. He wants everyone to be safe, so he watches out for them. He didn't used to, but more and more over the years, he has. I've been glad; it's the right thing to do." She was filling a second plate for Sionnach. "I think it's smart too. Both the Summer Queen and the Winter Queen used to be mortal."

If not for the fact that Rika was a faery discussing faery

politics in a cave, the quiet gathering of food would seem normal. Sometimes it was easy to see the mortal girl that she had been. Those glimpses of Rika were enchanting in a way that her Otherness wasn't. He didn't mind that she was fey, didn't want her to change, but the world she lived in was a little alien and unsettling. Knowing that an entire civilization existed hidden within his own left him with a sense of peril that he wished he didn't have. Until Rika, the desert had seemed safe—potentially harsh and filled with natural dangers, but those weren't threats with motive. Snakes didn't bite with malice; the sun didn't create heatstroke with intent.

Except according to Shy and Rika, the sun sometimes did just that when it was a manifestation of the Summer King . . . who is my girlfriend's ex.

Jayce shook his head at the oddity that was now a part of his life and then followed Rika back into the main chamber. Sionnach had been dozing. He looked up at them drowsily, eyes half-lidded. Even injured and still, the fox faery had something of the feral animal that Rika didn't.

"The other problem is that Maili has taken some issue with Shy, so . . ." Rika's words faded away when she noticed Sionnach blinking sleepily. "Sorry."

Jayce handed the faery a plate of food while Rika balanced her own plate on the vaguely table-shaped rock outcropping. "Why does Maili have issue with you?"

"It was inevitable." Sionnach suddenly looked uncomfortable, not meeting Rika's eyes.

"Why, Sionnach?"

"Seriously, Rika . . ."

"A girl," Jayce said in relief. The injured faery might have feelings for Rika, but he obviously also had someone else in his life that he hadn't told Rika about. "There's a girl."

"No." Rika laughed. "Shy doesn't do relationships, so that's not it. So what is it?"

After a long moment of silence, Sionnach asked, "Why do you say that?"

"Because you flirt with Rika to get her to do what you want, but you *say* you aren't interested in pursuing her that way, right?" Jayce flashed Sionnach a smile, half daring him to admit that he hadn't been honest with Rika about his feelings but half hoping the faery would keep his secret. He admitted to himself that he felt threatened by the history the two faeries shared, but they both insisted that there was nothing more. Jayce hoped his expression was not too revealing as he added, "And because a girl being involved seems like the only thing you'd be hesitant to admit."

"Shy?" Rika sounded puzzled.

"So maybe there is a girl. . . ." Sionnach sat up straighter in the bed. "I spent some time with a mortal lately, but it'll pass. I've never been one for relationships, Rika. Everyone knows that."

"But?" Jayce prompted, enjoying watching him squirm.

"But I told Maili and the rest that we ought to be a bit less invasive with the mortals and maybe consider being more respectful. She thinks it's because of my mortal."

Sionnach looked defensive, tilting his chin upward and staring directly at Jayce, as he continued, "I think treating mortals like toys is just not where we need to be. The world's changed and—"

"So have you. Good idea," Jayce interjected with a faux-somber look.

Rika looked stunned and a little speechless.

"It's not just because of Caris— . . . the mortal," Sionnach added hurriedly with a look at Rika. "Now that the Summer King has power for the first time in centuries, there will be trouble. He'll be trying to be strong enough to overpower the Winter Court."

"So it's about Keenan? Or mortals?" she asked.

"Both. I said that he'd come messing around. He has already. He's always been fond of mortals, so I figured we'd avoid trouble by treating them better. It wasn't because of Carissa. It's you too." The fox faery's voice dropped with his last admission, and Jayce felt a little sorry for him.

"Me?" Rika sounded like she didn't know if she should cry or hug him.

"I saw when you were a mortal, princess." Sionnach looked heartbroken. "I hated what he did, but then I knew you and . . ."

Rika stepped toward Sionnach. "That's why you became my friend. Because of what I was before?"

"Not just that," Sionnach said.

Jayce watched them, not with jealousy but with curiosity. Whatever the two faeries shared needed to be discussed.

Jayce suspected that Sionnach had manipulated his relationship with Rika—and he suspected that the fox faery had far deeper feelings for her than he admitted to any of them. The same history that made the two faeries friends was what had kept them from having a relationship. Jayce picked up his sketch pad and began drawing Sionnach and Rika.

Rika leaned over and kissed Sionnach's forehead. "So you fought over mortals."

"Not entirely. I'm the Alpha; I imposed some rules." Sionnach took her hand, squeezed it, and then gave her a mischievous look. "Some of the others objected to my suggestions."

"Objected?" Rika echoed. "You were *stabbed*. That's not objecting to suggestions."

Rika paced away, her mood turned from sad to angry in a moment. "I'll go to her and explain—"

"Explain? Princess, *explain* is a verbal thing. I think you mean *beat*."

"I can use words."

"'Can' and 'will' aren't the same." Sionnach turned to Jayce. "Faeries can't lie. You need to listen carefully to what we say and don't say."

"Oh, I have been," Jayce said levelly.

Sionnach smiled approvingly at him like he was a good pupil, but there was a glint in the fox faery's eyes that made clear that he realized what Jayce wasn't saying. Rika, however, was oblivious to the undercurrents in the conversation.

"She has it coming," Rika muttered.

"You know, I never even said it was Maili." Sionnach's

eyes widened in false innocence. "Maybe it was—"

"*Was* it Maili?" Rika interrupted.

"Well, yes."

"So tell me why I shouldn't go explain that she best not be so stupid in the future?"

There was an extended pause where the two faeries faced off, and Jayce wasn't entirely sure what was going on then. Their moods had changed abruptly. It had been a seemingly mild conversation, but suddenly, Rika looked more menacing than he'd seen so far. Her chin was up, her shoulders squared. Sionnach, even though he was in a bed, still looked fierce enough that cowering might be wise.

"Because if you do and she knocks you down, we are without recourse," Sionnach said gently. His lighter attitude vanished, and Jayce finally glimpsed the faery who was strong enough to keep order in the desert. He and Rika matched each other in subtle ways, looking fierce and projecting a heightened sense of Otherness. They seemed like two animals vying for control, and Jayce realized that to some degree that was exactly what was happening. He was all but invisible to them as they tried to establish which of them was in charge here.

Sionnach held Rika's gaze and added, "And I really dislike the Summer King . . . almost as much as you do."

At that, Rika deflated. "She *stabbed* you, Shy. I can't just ignore that."

He held out a hand. Rika went to him, took his hand, and sat on the cave floor.

"And we'll deal with her, but not now. Not when doing

so would leave you, Jayce, me and . . . all the others vulnerable. I cannot be Alpha right now. *You* can. You could even if I wasn't injured. Although you back down from me every time you start to challenge me, everyone in this room—most everyone in the desert—knows that you are stronger *if you want to be*." He used their combined hands to catch the underside of her chin and forced her to look at him. "You can't be Alpha if you back down, and I'm injured. We need to be smart about this. Maili's treacherous. If you fall, she's the next strongest here. She's not what we want in power even for a breath. Please?"

"For now. If I'm strong enough—"

"You are beyond strong, but you're not cruel enough, princess," Sionnach interrupted.

"You underestimate me, Shy. I think I'm quite able to be cruel."

"Are you sure enough to risk all of our safety on that belief?"

"No." Her gaze dropped. "Fine. I won't go looking for trouble. Yet."

"Good." Then the fierce faery who had just convinced Rika she was strong enough to be Alpha, yet also convinced her to bow to his wishes, fastened his gaze on Jayce. It wasn't an entirely friendly look. "There's a salve I brought for Jayce, Rika."

She stilled, her entire body tight and tense, but her voice sounded calm as she said, "There are rules, Shy."

"None higher than us out here," he countered. "He's no

use to me if he's unable to see what's around him."

"Right here, Sionnach," Jayce interjected. "And being of use to you isn't my top priority." He glanced at Rika, who looked increasingly nervous. "What's the salve for?"

"Seeing," she whispered.

Jayce waited, knowing that there was obviously more to it than what she'd said. He knew that faeries could be invisible to humans and were inaudible when they couldn't be seen. So, the obvious meaning was that the salve would let him see them. When neither of them spoke further, he prompted, "*And?*"

Sionnach waved his hand, earning a glare from Rika.

"Giving a mortal the Sight is not something we're to do," she said in a shaky voice as she stood and walked over to Jayce. "It's risky for mortals too. Some of the courts take mortals who can see them, those born with the Sight. Others just take the mortals' eyes."

Jayce wrapped an arm around her, but didn't answer. He wasn't sure he was ready for that particular risk, but he would rather discuss it away from Sionnach.

When Jayce didn't reply to Rika's words on the Sight, Sionnach suggested, "Why don't you two go do something more fun? All this maudlin business isn't particular romantic."

Jayce shrugged and said, "Call if you need us."

Sionnach held Jayce's gaze. "I do need you both."

"For now, we're both here," Jayce agreed mildly. He wasn't committing to anything more than that. He liked

Rika, but he didn't trust Sionnach or know how he felt about a path that included being a potential target for faeries who were willing to cut up people's eyes.

"I still get to be the one to knock the arrogance out of her," Rika interjected.

Jayce answered even though she had been talking to Sionnach. "You're the only one able to. I'm human, and *he's* obviously not tough enough—"

Sionnach's bark of laughter stilled Jayce's words. "I might like you, Jayce." Then he gave Rika a very serious look. "It would be a joy to watch you explain the error of her ways when the time is right."

"Soon," Rika added. "You'll be well soon and then—"

"And then we'll remind her that the most dangerous faery in the desert is you. . . . Now that you aren't in seclusion."

Jayce shivered at the way Sionnach smiled at them as they left the cave. The injured faery was clearly manipulative, but Rika seemed oblivious to it and Jayce wasn't entirely sure he objected. Whatever Sionnach's endgame was, for now he'd manipulated things so that Jayce was with the most interesting girl he'd ever met. It was hard to object to that.

Chapter 15

Rika wished she could have talked to Sionnach without Jayce there, but she admitted to herself that she wouldn't have felt the need to confront Sionnach without her mortal boyfriend's influence. He saw Sionnach without the filter of friendship and gratitude, and in doing so, he enabled her to see the fox faery more truly. While she might have been able to understand objectively that Sionnach was impish and unreliable in his way, she also trusted him as she'd trusted no one else in her life. She saw some of his flaws, but tended to overlook many of them.

She and Jayce followed the passageway to the room with her murals. They both kept art supplies in the chamber now. There were easels and wooden crates with jars of paints nestled in straw. She'd only ever let Sionnach and Jayce into this room, and only Jayce had slept there. Quietly, they both rolled out their sleeping bags.

"We could stay in the room where Sionnach is," Jayce

offered quietly. "If you need to hear him so you can take care of him, I mean."

"I can hear him just fine from here." Rika ducked her head, bashful even now. "And I wanted to be with only you."

Jayce kissed her and then said, "I like that plan."

"You don't have to use the salve," she said gently, moving away from him and not meeting his eyes. "They—*we*—aren't all good. Seeing them is dangerous, so you might be safer without the Sight."

Her words skirted near enough to a lie that she felt them like physical things rolling over her tongue. *Was he safer?* Maili had already stabbed Sionnach, and she'd shoved Jayce off a cliff. Maili was just one faery, though. If the court fey knew of a mortal with the Sight, they might come looking for him.

The Summer Queen had the Sight when she was mortal.

Rika didn't know if the new queen's mortal life would change how things were done, and even so, she was one faery regent in a world of centuries-old creatures with traditions even older than they were. She stared at Jayce, struggling with what and how to tell him without making herself sound like a monster too.

He stepped closer to her, reached out, and stroked her face. "I'll do it. I can pretend not to see them if I have to. It makes it easier on you if I can see threats near me, right?"

She nodded.

"Tomorrow then." He wrapped his arms around her. He comforted her, erased her nervousness, and it took but a moment.

Rika motioned toward a blank section of the cave and offered, "You could do one of the open spots if you wanted."

"I'd feel weird defacing—" He stopped himself. "Not that what *you* did was . . . I mean—"

"I've lived here for a *very* long time. I didn't have access to many other supplies when I came here. Most faeries can't create art." She shrugged, trying not to make too much of her difference even though it was something that filled her with pride.

"Why can you create?"

"Because I used to be human, I guess." She looked at the bit of the wall visible in the firelight. "I don't know what I'd have done without my art."

He stepped away from the sleeping bag and stood nearer to her, his gaze taking in the portraits on the wall. Miners and farmers stared back at them as if the past could look into the present. Buildings filled the spaces around them; most were ones that had long since fallen under the weight of time and nature. "What was it like here? When you came?"

"Emptier. There were some humans here already, but the others that came and built small mortal towns were often violent." She thought about other faces and places long gone, of a home she'd known on another continent, of other towns that she'd visited before the desert. There she'd felt too crowded by the mortals that she was no longer like. Here in the desert, she'd discovered open spaces. Even so, the people had frightened her. She admitted, "Some of the people who came here were interesting for a heartbeat or two, but I stayed in the cave a lot."

"And the faeries?"

"Those too weak to survive the growing winter out in the rest of the world or trying to escape notice or hoping for autonomy . . . they came here." She gave him a wry smile. "Much like the mortals, I suppose—seeking freedom, power, or escape."

He didn't comment, waiting in that way of his that made her want to keep talking, that made her think that her words were interesting.

"Much like me, too," she confessed.

"Which were you seeking?"

"Probably all of it—freedom, power, and escape." She nestled closer to him, thinking to herself that she still sought escape and freedom, but now she sought it in Jayce's arms. When she'd started dating him, when he had looked at her and seen her, she'd thought she could have everything she wanted with him. Tonight, though, thinking about Maili had made her accept that she hadn't been truthful with herself for a long time. Quietly, she told him, "I didn't admit that I wanted power back then. I didn't need to because Shy had the power, and he was no threat to me."

"And now?" he prompted, and she realized that he *knew*. He had seen her confrontation with Sionnach, a fight that could've easily become a challenge for Alpha.

"Now I need to keep Maili from having power and keep Keenan from messing with my freedom."

Rika needed to go out into the desert and let the faeries see her. Since Sionnach wasn't up to it, they'd decided that she needed to be the reminder that there were faeries stronger than Maili. That meant leaving Jayce behind for his safety. Walking through the desert had always helped clear Rika's mind, but she now felt strangely off-kilter being alone. Being with Jayce and Sionnach lately had reminded her that she used to like being around others. Years ago, the solitary life she'd led when she first became fey had been hard, more so because she'd never been on her own until then, even *more* so because she'd wanted to be with Keenan in the throng of frolicking faeries that made up the Summer Court. Over time, though, she'd grown accustomed to isolation and to the quiet that came with being the Winter Girl, but she'd never *chosen* that life. She admitted now that choosing to be alone in the desert may have been a way to protect herself from the devastation that she'd felt when her loneliness had been beyond her control. If one chose to be alone, it was easier than being forced into it—at least that was what she'd told herself.

As she walked, she saw humans scaling the rocks. In the desert, climbers were as common as coyotes. They were part of the landscape. Mortals from all over came to the Mojave to climb and to hike. She'd learned not to notice them overmuch. These mortals were surrounded by faeries though, and she couldn't help but think of how Jayce had fallen.

In a blur of motion, she ran toward them. "Back off."

The mortals, of course, didn't react: this time, she'd remembered to stay invisible.

A faery who looked very much like a barrel cactus, squat and whisker-covered, stepped into her path. "Since when is it your business what we do?"

"Since I decided it was."

In a nearby crevice in the rock, Maili watched. Rika opted not to look her way yet since she had, in essence, promised Sionnach that she'd not go looking for trouble. She was doing as she'd agreed, but if Maili began a confrontation, Rika would have to respond. No one could expect anything different.

Instead of answering, one of the faeries shoved a human. It wasn't a true attack; the boy was low enough to the ground that it wasn't much of a fall. At most, the boy would be bruised and scraped.

"Don't. Do. That." Rika bit off each word, but she didn't strike anyone. She still wanted Sionnach to be the Alpha here. Meting out physical punishments was an Alpha's obligation and right, not hers. Unless she was the Alpha, all Rika was rightly able to do was respond to aggression.

"You shouldn't meddle," Maili said as she stepped out of her hiding place. In her hands were manacles, and since she wore leather gloves that stretched up to her elbows to protect her from the metal, Rika knew that the restraints were fashioned of steel or iron.

The air became heavy with dust, impairing her vision. She shook her head and blinked against the dust. "Your inability to fight fair is embarrassing."

As she clambered up the rocks, she saw the source of the dust: a pair of faeries tossed sand into the air while another with balloon-ish cheeks exhaled in big gasps. From behind her another faery tackled her, piercing her skin with the thin needles that covered him. She pulled her knee up hard, and when his grip loosened, she slammed her head into his face.

Several more faeries launched themselves toward the fight immediately. At least two were those she'd often seen at Maili's side, ones she'd fought a few weeks ago in town. Two others, one male and one female, also jumped into the fray.

Rika wasn't fragile, but her odds were slim against six faeries during a dust storm. Still, she wasn't going to accept defeat easily. She kicked the leg of one of the largest faeries, snapping his knee backward, and headbutted another one of those not covered in thorns.

After only a few moments, though, she was overwhelmed. Between the sand blinding her and the sheer number of them, Maili's group of faeries had her pinned to the ground. Quickly, Maili snapped the manacles closed on Rika's ankles and then her wrists.

As soon as Maili had the restraints in place, she stepped back, and the other faeries started releasing Rika.

She promptly smashed her bound hands into another faery's face. She fell back to the ground, and at the same time, she kicked her legs up and yanked another faery down with her feet. She might be down, but that didn't mean she was done fighting.

"Stop!" Maili snarled as she snatched hold of Rika and jerked her to her feet with the manacles that now bound Rika's wrists.

Rika slammed her head upward as hard as she could, catching Maili under the chin.

"I said *stop*!" Maili wrenched the chain downward, causing Rika to stumble.

It took concentration not to wince from the metal burning her skin or to fall from the limited movement still allowed by her bound ankles. Rika shook her hair out of her face, dabbed at her bleeding mouth with her upper arm, and stared directly at Maili. "You get stupider by the week."

The other faeries shuffled nervously.

"I told Shy I wouldn't attack you." Rika kept her voice almost conversational as she took a somewhat steady step toward Maili.

Foolishly, Maili didn't back up. The others, however, did.

"Do you honestly think I'll forgive this?" Rika asked.

Maili still didn't move.

"You shouldn't get involved," Rika said, looking briefly at the other faeries, hoping that they had the sense to leave. She could still take Maili, but not all of them, especially not bound. She kept her voice level and said, "Stop backing her, and I'll forgive you. I understand boredom."

No one spoke, but they grew even more still, a thing Rika wouldn't have thought possible many years ago.

"If you cross me, if you cross Shy," Rika continued hopefully, "you won't be staying in my desert much longer."

At that, Maili laughed. *"Your desert?"*

"Mine," Rika reiterated.

Maili made a disgusted sound—and shoved a syringe into Rika's arm.

When Rika woke, manacles still restrained her. Her wrists were red, and one was bleeding from her resisting even while only semiconscious. She looked around and realized that she was in an alley. Several rusted fire escapes jutted out from the buildings, and she was now suspended from one of them. Her feet dangled down to brush the ground, but she had very little slack in the chains.

"Are you blind?" Maili's voice drew her attention. The faery who'd trapped her was sitting on a wooden crate out of reach. In her hand she held the end of a cord that was attached to the chains holding Rika. "*Shy* is playing you."

Rika ignored the attempt at conversation and tugged her arms forward, causing her wrist to bleed more freely. "This is stupid—even for you."

"Do you think he's any different than the Summer King? They both use their charms to make you pliable." Maili jerked on the cord, pulling the chain taut. The steel cuffs jerked Rika's arms back over her head. "At his request, I *helped* him push you toward the mortal."

"*What?* Why?" Rika stared at Maili, trying to understand why the faery would entrap her and tell her such things. She hadn't expected to be killed or any such thing. Murder was extreme for faeries, even one so unstable as Maili. Extended torture wasn't unheard of; some courts thrived on such things. Being captured to *talk*, however, was peculiar.

When Maili said nothing else, Rika said, "Why would he do that?"

Maili's arrogant expression vanished, but then quickly returned. "What difference does it make?"

"You don't *know* why." Rika felt a surge of relief at that. Unfortunately, she also felt a burst of worry. Faeries couldn't lie outright, so Maili had known something Rika hadn't known. *Why would Shy push me toward Jayce?* It didn't make sense.

It also wasn't her primary problem just then. She focused her attention on Maili, but studied her surroundings casually too. There weren't any faeries nearby to help Rika, and Maili was too far away to attack—plus there was the matter of the steel restraints that were currently searing Rika's skin.

Maili seemed lost in her thoughts too. She scowled briefly and then said, "He misled you. He treats us different now. Making new rules. Trying to control us. Solitaries don't do that. His being Alpha doesn't mean he's a king."

Rika rattled her chains. "*He* didn't attack me though, did he? He didn't chain me up with poison binding my skin."

"Are you really going to let him get away with this?" Maili came close enough now that Rika could almost reach her. In doing so, Maili had allowed the chains to get slack.

"I don't know. Sionnach is the only faery out here who's made me any offers. No one else has even wanted to talk, but I'd listen if you had a better offer," Rika said misleadingly as she tried to keep her temper hidden. For a brief moment, she was grateful for the years she'd spent twisting her words and learning to hide her emotions around court fey.

Maili looked at Rika pensively.

"And do I truly need to be shackled to talk?" She shook one arm a bit, causing the chain to shiver. "I'm not opposed to talking, but not like this."

"You understand, don't you?" Maili's eyes widened in excitement. "He's trying to make us into something we aren't. We make our own way. Humans are fair game. So what if a few of them get broken. . . ."

Rika tilted her head and gave Maili an attentive look. "It has always been that way."

"Exactly." Maili let the chains fall looser still. "Keenan's people tell me we can have our freedom still . . . that it won't be any different. . . ."

"So you're going to swear to him?"

"No, I'm not, but if they'll let me break Sionnach and be independent, convincing the others to offer the Summer King a little obedience here and there isn't so bad. I'll become Alpha. Sionnach will either obey or leave. The ones I decide need extra leashing will be forced to swear fealty to the Summer King."

"He's not trustworthy," Rika said mildly.

"Exactly. That's why I need you to help me get rid of him." Maili smiled at Rika like she'd given a particularly insightful answer.

Her chains were finally sagging enough that she could

punch Maili—so she did. Then she grabbed her and pulled her close, spinning her so that her back was to Rika's chest. To anyone watching it would look like Rika was embracing her.

"I meant that *Keenan* isn't trustworthy," Rika corrected.

Maili struggled as Rika choked her with the chains until she was unconscious. Then, holding Maili's limp form in one arm, she used her other hand to go through Maili's pockets until she found the keys. It was not a quick or easy process, but it worked. She retrieved the key and let Maili slump to the ground, alive but not conscious.

"Of course, Shy isn't trustworthy either," Rika told the unconscious faery. "But he also isn't trying to steal everyone's freedom."

She unlocked the manacles, put them on Maili, and left her chained up to the fire escape.

Then Rika pocketed the keys and walked away. When she reached the end of the alley and stepped out, Maili's helpers stared at her. None of them moved to attack her now. They weren't malicious. Being a solitary faery meant obeying those stronger; it meant making allegiances that faded when power shifted.

"Don't be stupid," she cautioned them. "Scratch that. Don't be any stupider than you've already been. Following Maili or believing her theories about trusting the Summer King would be a bad idea."

One of them started to attempt to explain. "Maili said . . . but we didn't want to hurt you. It's just that Maili said—"

"She's not the strongest faery in the desert," Rika interjected. "Neither is Shy. I am."

They didn't reply, but there was nothing truthful they could say. Even those who'd never lived among the court fey knew about the curse. Many of the solitary fey in the desert were those who had fled there to escape the cold that had become so pervasive in much of the world because of the curse. Knowing about the curse also meant that they knew that the former Winter Girls were strong, much stronger than fey who'd hidden in the desert.

"I'm not going to be so forgiving in the future if you keep helping her—or if you injure humans." Rika looked at them each in turn. "I was human a long time ago. It would be wise to remember that next time you think about harassing mortals."

Some of them nodded; others looked surly. It didn't matter if they agreed with her rule, though. They would obey her. If not, she'd remind them of how strong she really was. That wasn't the fate she'd sought, but she wasn't going to let anyone push her around again.

When Rika returned to her home, she went to the cavern where Jayce and Sionnach were playing a game. They both looked up at her when she entered. She barely nodded at Jayce. She was afraid that if she spoke at all, her anger at Sionnach would boil over. She couldn't remember ever feeling so foolish with anyone but Keenan. The first faery she'd trusted since the Summer King, the first faery in the desert she'd thought of as a friend, and he'd used her.

"You!" She poked Sionnach in the chest. "How dare you manipulate me?"

"So you know," he said levelly.

"Get out, Sionnach. Now."

He didn't move. However, Jayce quietly turned away from them, giving her the illusion of privacy. Rika wasn't sure she could stay in the same space with Sionnach. She turned and kept walking, heading back to her bed, not sure of much other than the need to curl into her nest until her temper was cooled.

Sionnach didn't have the sense to let her do that. He followed her, not just into the room but close enough that he now stood directly in front of her. He caught her gaze and simply stared at her for a moment, not speaking or moving. In all the years she'd known him, she'd never been as furious as she was right then, and he just stood there staring at her.

Rika shoved him. "What were you thinking? I trusted you."

"I made some calculated risks when I knew Maili had gone to *Keenan*." His voice grew louder as he spoke. "Don't you understand? He's—" Suddenly, Sionnach's words broke off. He walked away, pacing as he did when he was tense or cornered, and when he continued, his voice was level. "I don't want to fight with you. I had a plan, but I needed time before I could explain it all to you."

"Maili told me. So nice to be a pawn again." Rika

watched him as she told him about being trapped and chained up. She stared at him as she told him everything Maili had said.

Fear was plain on Sionnach's face, but he said nothing.

"You aren't denying any of it," she said quietly.

"Would you believe me?" he asked just as quietly.

"So Jayce was what? A distraction? A prize?" She felt a familiar tangle of embarrassment and anger. She'd let Sionnach know that she'd cared for Jayce, let him see that she wanted so desperately just to be loved that she'd taken to following a mortal boy around.

Sionnach still said nothing in his defense, nothing to explain away his actions or even ask about Maili's fate or her injuries. He simply stared at her silently.

"How *could* you do this to me?" She repeated the one question that had been playing over and over in her mind since Maili's revelations.

Finally, Sionnach looked as furious as Rika felt, anger replacing the fear in his eyes. "You didn't leave me a lot of options. I've waited for *years* for you to find a reason to come out of your gloom and look at the world. You did *nothing*. You stayed here in the dark and pouted. Caring for someone . . . it makes you see what matters." His fox tail had flicked madly behind him while he spoke, and then all at once, it stopped. He stilled completely and said only, "I care about you."

Rika knew that tears were streaking down her cheeks, knew that he saw them and felt guilty for it, but none of that changed anything. He'd manipulated her. She walked up to him, standing closer than she'd ever stood when they'd argued, and folded her arms over her chest. "Not enough to make you honest though."

Sionnach didn't back down. "Jayce is good for you. Look how happy you've been lately. I just moved a few pieces so you'd have to act on it. Once you were with him, I knew you'd want to make things safer in the desert."

"You really aren't any different than Keenan, are you?" Tears dripped down her cheeks, falling onto her chest and crossed arms. She didn't wipe away her tears, afraid that if she stopped holding on to herself she'd strike Sionnach.

"You know that's not true, Rika," he said. "I heard about Keenan being unbound. I tried to make changes so we weren't doing things that would attract his attention too soon, but I wasn't strong enough to handle it alone if he came here . . . and he did. I needed help. You're stronger, and if we work together—if we act like *friends*—we can keep the desert safe." Sionnach reached out as if to wipe her tears away.

She slapped his hand. "Friends don't manipulate one another."

"I needed you, and you needed someone who—"

"What about letting *me* decide what I need?"

"You weren't deciding *anything*." His anger returned, and his tail swished rapidly behind him again.

"So that makes it right to manipulate me?"

"Politics, love, passion—giving Jayce to you solved so many things." He reached out again, but didn't touch her. "This is best for everyone."

"So I'm simply to be okay with being manipulated for your *plans*?"

"I care for you enough to want you happy, and I love my freedom enough to want to—"

"To want to use me." Rika turned and walked into the main room, where Jayce was waiting. He didn't say anything, but he'd obviously heard all of it. After only a moment, he opened his arms, and she went into his embrace.

She buried her face against him and cried.

After her sobs let up, he wiped the tears from her cheeks, but didn't press her to talk. Somewhere inside her home, Sionnach quietly waited, but he didn't seek her out and force her to speak either.

Rika rested her head on Jayce's shoulder, and they sat there silently until evening fell. Jayce didn't chastise her for the mess he'd been drawn into because of her. She waited for him to leave, grateful that he hadn't walked out while she and Sionnach argued.

Finally, Rika went to a trunk and retrieved an oft-folded and refolded letter. She smoothed it out and carried it to Jayce. "Can you dial this number before you go?"

He pulled out his cell phone, put it on speakerphone, and dialed.

Through the phone, a cold voice answered, "Hello."

"I need to speak to Donia. This is Rika."

Then Donia's voice came over the line: "Rika? Are you okay?"

"I need your help. Can I see you?"

Donia's laughter was short but genuinely amused. "Not in the desert. You could come to me though."

"I'm on my way." Rika waited until Donia disconnected, and then she went to collect her things to travel before Sionnach could notice her departure.

Chapter 16

"Where is that salve?" Jayce asked as she was shoving things into her bag.

Rika said nothing at first. She thought it through one more time. Jayce was at risk with or without the Sight. If he had the ability to see the fey when they were invisible to mortals, he was in danger of having his eyes gouged out. If he didn't have the ability to see them, he was unable to see those that could hurt him.

"Rika?"

"You can't let the court fey know that you can see them without their consent." She stopped packing and stared at him. "Can you be *sure* you can do that for the rest of your life?"

Jayce paused, his expression flickering between thoughtful and determined. After a few moments, he said, "There are creatures all around me that I can only see when they allow it. I want to see the whole world because . . . it seems wrong *not* to see, and I don't want to be blind to threats."

Silently, Rika retrieved the tiny pot of salve from her bag. She'd stuffed it in there before anything else, figuring it was best to carry it with them just in case they needed it. Jayce watched her with a solemn gaze that altered only briefly when he saw where the salve had been.

Carefully, she dabbed the salve onto her fingertip and then applied it to his eyes. She hoped that Sionnach had made it correctly, had found the right recipe, had thought this through. Even now, when she was furious with him, she trusted him enough to use the ointment he'd given them.

Jayce blinked a little, stared at her, and then murmured, "You look the same."

"I used to be human," she reminded him.

He nodded, and they finished gathering their things to travel.

Once they were in the desert, she was relieved that he could contain his reaction to the faeries that were now visible to him. He muttered "Wow," but he didn't stare at them and his soft exclamation could've been in reference to anything. He squeezed her hand a couple of times, either in excitement or nervousness, but in all, he hid his reaction to seeing the world revealed in a new light. She hadn't been anywhere near that subtle in her responses when she'd first seen the creatures that lived hidden all around mortals. Then again, she'd also just *become* such a creature, so her own responses were heightened by emotions he didn't have to experience.

"It's amazing," he said, almost reverently. His gaze drifted across the desert, and anyone watching could easily think he was referring to the cacti and cliffs.

"Deadly too," she reminded him.

"My girlfriend is ruling the desert, right?"

"More or less."

"Then I feel pretty safe," he told her. "You can keep me safe."

Admittedly, he had a point. Whether she took Alpha from Sionnach—which she certainly could if she wanted to—or accepted his repeated offered to share it with him, she would be able to keep Jayce safe from the fey here. She could order them not to reveal his Sight. Realizing that went far to easing her worries.

"Only here though," she cautioned. "Outside the desert, I have no power."

He nodded.

Rika and Jayce were silent as they crossed the desert. There were more things to discuss than she knew how to handle. The hardest of which just then was that she was going to tell Jayce he couldn't come with her to see the Winter Queen. There were rules in dealing with the courts, and she wasn't foolish enough to expect that all of those rules would vanish because she'd known Donia when she wasn't yet a queen. Unfortunately, Rika wasn't convinced that leaving Jayce in the desert was ideal either. Things were increasingly unsettled in the wake of the attack on Sionnach, and before that Keenan's visit, and earlier still, the

Summer King's assumption of his full power. The solitary faeries might be outside the courts, but that didn't mean they were untouched by the events that happened within the courts. They all knew trouble was brewing. The only question was if they could avoid the worst of it.

Beside her, Jayce looked pensive, and while she couldn't solve all of the problems facing the solitaries, she hoped she could sort out whatever was worrying her mortal boyfriend.

Rika took his hand as they walked. "What are you thinking?"

"I'm a part of your world now, Rika, just as you are a part of mine." Jayce's expression became the already-familiar determined one that told her that he was going to say something he didn't expect her to like. Quietly, he said, "I'm not like Keenan . . . *or* like Sionnach."

Rika looked startled. "I know."

"So everything will be okay."

She had to look away. Seeing him so open, so unlike the fey, made it hard to refuse whatever he wanted—especially right now. As her gaze darted around the desert, she could see a dozen or so faeries peering out at her from behind rocks. They weren't the ones who had seen her with Maili, and by the curious way they watched her, it was clear that they hadn't heard about her altercation with Maili. They were simply acting as they always did, watching and teasing. They came out of hiding to approach her.

"Ooooh, she's leaving."

"With her pet."

"Running away with a *mortal*."

Rika shook her head before she corrected them. "I'm not leaving. I'll be back."

"Mortals aren't all bad," a faery muttered.

The others all paused to stare at the faery who'd just spoken such an unusual thing out here in the desert. Rika smiled at him approvingly. The desert fey weren't a bad lot; they simply needed to learn some new ideas.

Jayce glanced at her questioningly, and she nodded.

"*Or* just pets," Jayce casually added.

In a surge of movement surprisingly quick in the mid-day heat, the faeries skittered away from Rika and Jayce. Their expressions were clouded with mistrust and doubt as they stared at the mortal boy beside her. Rika couldn't truly blame them; it *was* unusual to be seen by mortals. There were those rare few born with faery Sight, but she couldn't recall the last time she'd seen such a mortal.

"He *sees* us," one faery accused.

With more patience that she wanted to have, Rika put her hands on her hips. "I gave him faery Sight. It seemed only fair."

The faeries scurried away muttering about her disregard for the rules, and Rika was momentarily glad that the faery regent she was going to see that day had reputedly broken that very same rule recently—and had done so for the new Summer Queen's beloved. If the regents were allowing mortals to have the Sight, it was harder to argue that she shouldn't have done so.

Jayce draped his arm over her shoulders. "I'm not your pet, but I am yours. I know you're upset over what Sionnach did, but falling on you was the best thing that I ever did."

"You didn't fall. They *pushed* you," she corrected him. "Sionnach probably told them to do it. Solitaries are not civilized. They're manipulative."

"I know."

"And the same faery who helped Shy stabbed him."

"I know," he repeated.

"Maili tried to injure me earlier. She said all she wanted to do was talk, but she hurt me to do it." Rika moved away from him, hoping that distance from his touch would strengthen her resolve to leave him in the desert. She held up her bruised and burned wrists. "She did this."

"I *know*." Jayce followed her. "I listened when you explained it—and when you yelled at Shy. I heard it all, but I'm not giving up on you just because we were manipulated or because you're a faery."

"You should. You know that, don't you?"

"Don't let Shy or Keenan or any of them"—Jayce gestured into the direction the faeries went—"make you give up on us."

"Faeries can't keep mortals," Rika said sorrowfully. "And now that Shy . . . and Maili . . . and Keenan have put me in this position. . . ." She looked away, unable to bear the tangled frustration and determination in his expression.

"So tell me you'd be happier without me. Tell me you haven't had more fun these past few weeks than you have had in a very long time."

She looked back at him and admitted, "I can't, but I'll have responsibilities now. If I'm going to be Alpha or even co-Alpha, things will change. Maili won't be the only faery to challenge me. There will be fights, and I have to figure out what to do about Sionnach, and if Donia won't help, I need to deal with Keenan, and—"

"You'll be busier," he interrupted. "That's fine. You do your Alpha thing, and we'll date around your schedule of fighting rowdy faeries. It's not like I can't find things to do when you're busy: classes, skating, art, climbing. . . ." He caught her hands and pulled her closer. "I have a *life* of my own, you know? I just want to be a part of yours, too."

Rika shook her head. It sounded too easy, and she'd never exactly known a relationship to be easy. Maybe he was right though. With more hope than she'd felt since before Sionnach was stabbed and she was captured, she asked, "You're sure?"

"I've never been *more* sure." Jayce kissed her, giving her the reassurance that she needed.

When she pulled away, she kept hold of one of his hands. "Fine. Let's go see the Winter Queen then. With her help, I won't have to fight as often."

With his hand in hers, she began to run across the desert. The speed at which she could move was something that she'd cherished about being fey from the very beginning. At first, she'd needed that speed to better serve the last Winter Queen. She'd helped to freeze the earth, a painful process that hadn't ever gotten easier with time. Carrying some of the weight of winter inside a body was painful for anyone other than the Winter Queen. She'd done it as her punishment for trusting Keenan, the cost of being willing to cross the then Winter Queen, who had wanted no one to take the test. The only benefits of the curse were that she had been made fey—given speed and near-immortality—and those advantages were only conferred on the Winter Girls because without them, the girls would die when they took the test. Now, that same faery speed was simply a benefit that she could utilize for her own purposes. As they ran, the scenery blurred as they raced by cities, fields, and mountains, until they stopped in a busy street in front of a house that had featured in far too many of her nightmares.

The massive gray house before them had turrets and oddly shaped windows that were filled by faces of creatures that had once seemed stranger than she could've created in her darkest hours. Those same faeries were no longer a threat to her, but back then she'd been the Winter Girl cursed by the old Winter Queen, who had seemed to live to terrorize everyone.

The house seemed less ominous now even though faces still peered from the windows, and the yard was snow-draped despite it being spring. Rika's grasp on Jayce's hand tightened as they approached the iron fence that still wrapped around the property. She was briefly surprised that Donia hadn't had the poisonous metal removed, but with the upheaval between the courts, maybe that touch of menace was wise. Winter was still the strongest of the courts, even though Summer was recently unbound. A reminder that Donia could be a force to fear was a good move politically.

"Everything should be fine," Rika whispered, but she still shivered as she stepped through the gate and onto the elegantly curved sidewalk that wound between trees that were bowing under the weight of snow and ice. She wasn't sure that everything *would* be fine. An awful lot of things were very *not* fine in her life, but she'd known Donia since the girl was a mortal. Like Rika, Donia had been one of the unlucky girls who had caught the then–bound Summer King's attention. Rika had done all she could to convince her not to take the test. Afterward, she'd worked hard to hide her own bitterness from Donia, hoping that she could ease the newly fey girl's pain by creating the illusion that one day forgiveness and freedom would come. Donia had been the last Winter Girl, though. Recently, she had been freed from the curse and replaced Beira, the Winter Queen who had made them all suffer for so long. Of all the faeries Rika had met, none were so easily trusted as the former Winter Girls. None of them spent much time together, choosing instead to forge new lives, but they all helped when one of their sisters needed them. Rika would be surprised if Donia refused her offer—especially when what she'd come to propose would also be an asset to the new queen.

CHAPTER 17

As Rika approached her house, Donia felt a twinge of envy. The former Winter Girl was holding the hand of a mortal boy. Like the Summer Queen and her mortal, Rika had someone at her side. Of late, even the Dark King had found a way to be reunited with the one he loved. It was only the High Queen and the Winter Queen who were without partners, and even the High Queen had found some affection. For her it was creating a son. So in reality, it was only Donia who remained without love, just as she had been when she was the Winter Girl. For a person who had risked everything for love, who had lost her mortality and then almost given her life for the one she loved, being deserted seemed an unreasonably cruel fate. It wasn't that Donia wanted any of them to lose *their* loved ones—she wasn't so heartless as her predecessor—she merely wished that she wasn't without her beloved. Keenan was and had always been the one faery she couldn't have, a faery who had only claimed his court because he'd found his rightful queen. *A queen who is not me.*

Many years ago, Donia had dreamed that she was the one he sought. Like Rika and numerous others, she'd thought that loving Keenan would be enough to break the curse that bound him. She'd believed that love really could conquer all. Now, she knew better. Maybe for Rika or the other former Winter Girls, there would be happy futures. Donia hoped so.

She smiled as she stood in the open doorway with Sasha, her white wolf, beside her. She lowered her hand to caress her constant companion behind his ears. He leaned against her affectionately.

At the foot of the stairs to Donia's house, Rika stopped, let go of the boy's hand, and stepped forward. Even now, so very crushable in front of a regent, the former Winter Girl stood unbending. Donia smiled at how familiar Rika's posture was: that strength was what had enabled them both to survive the curse.

"Hello, Rika." Donia's words were accompanied by a white cloud of frozen air.

"Sister," Rika greeted. She ascended the steps and held open her arms.

The boy stayed on the sidewalk behind her. He shoved his hands into his trouser pockets and shivered, but his gaze didn't leave Rika.

"Sisters always," Donia promised as she embraced Rika. They shared no blood, but as with the rest of the former

Winter Girls, there would always be an affection between them that no one other than a former Winter Girl would understand. Carrying ice and snow inside a body not made for such pain wasn't something that could be explained—nor would those who'd experienced it *want* to try to describe it. Some experiences were not meant to be spoken.

When Rika stepped back, she said, "You look healthier."

Donia shrugged delicately. "Ruling suits me better than . . . the other. Carrying the curse of Keenan's mistakes was unpleasant."

Rika shook her head. "We both survived though."

"And Beira didn't." Donia felt the storms fill her eyes and knew that they were snow white. A gust of icy air radiated from her skin, causing the trees to shiver and snow to fall from their branches in a brief flurried snowfall. Being around the other former Winter Girls stirred memories and emotions that they'd all rather forget. She suspected that was why they so rarely saw each other. Beira's curse had made so many people suffer, and it was harder to deny those memories when the person in front of you had similar ones.

"I'm glad she's dead." Rika shivered again.

Donia tried to keep her own chill reined in as she said, "She won't ever hurt any of us again. I'm the queen now."

"Was it horrible? Her death?"

Truthfully, Donia hadn't expected *that* question, but she wasn't surprised. Beira had devastated a lot of lives, and few faeries mourned her passing. No one had sought Donia out for details, and few faeries would be so bold as to ask for details from the reigning queen.

"It was," Donia said softly. She had lived for almost a century, but the day Beira had died and Donia had become Winter Queen was one of the memories that she still dreamed about more often than she'd like. Sometimes in the remembering, it felt like the moment was trapped forever in the now, as if—like the day when Donia had lost her mortality—it would never be an experience that she could relegate to memories.

The floor is already covered in spikes of ice; the furniture is well past broken. In the midst of the destruction, Beira stands like a beautiful nightmare. Despite the horror she has inflicted, Beira has always been lovely, dark hair and shocking red lips contrasting with the extreme pallor of ice.

She tilts her head inquiringly. "Do you think they'll be more upset if you're dead or still suffering?"

Donia is bleeding and exhausted, trying to rescue Seth—the mortal that the new Summer Queen loves. The boy is a strange one, brave in the face of the embodiment of Winter even after he's had one of his facial piercings ripped out. His dark hair falls over his face, hiding his expression in the moment.

"Decision, decisions," Beira murmurs as she walks over blades of ice, slowly and gracefully, as if she were entering the theater. She looks at Donia and Seth, trying to decide whom to torture next.

After a moment, she pulls Donia up by her hair and kisses both cheeks. Her frigid lips leave frost burn on Donia's skin. Being the Winter Girl gives her some tolerance of the ice, but Beira is *Winter. Since the last Summer King died over nine hundred years ago and the then newborn king was cursed, no one has been able to stand against her.*

"I believe I already told you what would happen to you, dearie," Beira whispers, and then she seals her lips to Donia's. The ice pours from the angry queen's lips into Donia's mouth. In moments, she will be frozen alive.

She doesn't see Seth until he throws himself at Beira.

The furious Winter Queen drops Donia, but she doesn't understand why until she sees the rusty iron sticking out of Beira's neck.

With surprising strength for a mortal—especially an injured one—he's attacked Beira, and the Winter Queen is not amused. She lashes out at Seth with a burst of ice and cold; the force of it slams him into a wall. Beira follows him in that too-fast-to-follow way.

"Do you think that little trinket will kill me?" She digs her fingers into the skin of his stomach and—using his ribs as a handle—jerks him to his feet.

He screams over and over, awful sounds that make Donia tremble, but she can't help him. She can't even lift her head from the floor. The mortal has risked his death to help her, but even that seems too little, too late. She feels the ice that Beira has exhaled into her body. It's killing her.

Beira removes her bony fingers from Seth's stomach, and he slides down the wall, slumping in a boneless pile.

Donia struggles to crawl to him as the ice slides down her throat, choking her, filling her lungs. She's not sure what she can do, but she wants to save him.

Beira doesn't attempt to stop her, but she doesn't need to.

Donia has barely managed to move. Her vision blurs, and she closes her eyes.

Donia has no idea how long she is motionless on the floor. She opens her eyes when a burst of heat stirs her.

Aislinn is there. The girl is no longer mortal. She's the queen that Keenan sought, and she's at his side now. They're both glowing so brightly that it hurts to see them. The newly ascended Summer Queen is holding Beira's arms as Keenan leans closer, his lips almost touching Beira's mouth.

Then he just breathes.

Sunlight pours onto her like some viscous fluid.

The Winter Queen struggles to turn her head and can't. She's held in place by the sunlit hands of the Summer King and Queen as she chokes on sunlight. The heat burns through Beira's throat; steam hisses from the cut.

When finally she is limp in their hands, Keenan steps away, and Aislinn lowers Beira's body to the floor.

The faery for whom Donia had long ago surrendered her mortality has killed the Winter Queen. He's broken the curse, found his queen and claimed his power. As he kneels at Donia's side, she wants to flinch from the heat of him even as she wants to kiss him one last time before death claims her. Instead, she becomes the new Winter Queen.

"Yes, Beira's death was horrible," Donia said. A tiny snow shower formed around her. Snowflakes fluttered to the ground like butterflies—slow and gentle in contrast to the remembered anger filling her now. She would say more, but not in front of a mortal.

"Good." Rika's expression held the sympathy that told

Donia that the faery heard more than the words Donia had uttered. Then Rika added, "Now, if Keenan suffers a bit, all will be well."

When Rika turned to her mortal, Donia fell back to the memories. The moments after the last Winter Queen's death were the hardest part of that day.

Keenan kneels on the floor and pulls Donia into his arms.

She has to cough before she can speak. "Beira really dead?"

He smiles, looking like every dream she's denied having. "She is."

"Seth?" It hurts to talk, her throat raw from the jagged pieces of ice she's swallowed.

"Seth's injured, but not dead." Keenan strokes her face, gently, as if she's something delicate and precious, as if she's the one who will share his throne. Sunlit tears run down his cheeks and drip onto her face, melting the ice that still clings to her. "I thought I'd lost you. I thought we were too late."

Even after all that had happened, Donia still believed that the Summer King was worth the pain, worth the curse, worth the death she thought she'd know that day. She had believed that for decades, but loving Keenan didn't mean she was blind to his faults. He was the careless, forgetful Summer. Even when he wasn't being willfully manipulative, he was still the embodiment of a season that thought first of pleasure and rarely of consequence—and whatever he'd done now had sent one of the former Winter Girls to Donia's doorstep.

She stepped to the side to allow Rika and her mortal to enter the house. She looked out into the street beyond her yard, where the world looked like summer. It was a visible demarcation, the line between the two seasons. Out in the world summer was growing, but within her yard it was always winter. He had his Summer Garden, and she had her Winter Garden. Their courts still needed a home when the other held sway over the world. Donia took a moment's comfort in the beautiful landscape—frost-covered lawn, trees bowed under the weight of snow and ice, unmarred fresh snow glistening.

Love doesn't mean being under his control. It doesn't mean giving in to his every whim or wish.

A former Winter Girl, especially one who had fled to the desert years ago, wouldn't come here to the home of the reigning Winter Queen without serious reason. Donia focused her attention on the summer street, and her wintery climate expanded beyond her yard. New buds on the trees froze as she looked upon them. *I won't surrender all of my power for you, even now,* she silently swore to the Summer King, who would no doubt be darkening her door soon. *I am your equal now, Keenan. Come fight with me.*

Then with the solemnity of early winter mornings, Donia turned away and resolutely closed the door.

Chapter 18

Far from the Winter Queen's home, Sionnach walked slowly through town with Carissa. He had spent several hours looking for Rika, checking all of her usual hideaways, but had been forced to admit defeat. She'd never been this angry with him, and he could admit—quietly, to himself—that he would be angry if he were in her position. Of course, he manipulated people and faeries as easily as he breathed, so he wouldn't end up in her position. Still, he could allow that she had grounds for her ire. He'd simply wait for her to calm down and return, and while he waited, he'd enjoy a date with the mortal girl . . . and try to ignore his injuries.

Carissa was, like so many young mortal women, full of dreams and passions. It's why faeries found them so alluring. Something about the impermanence of mortals seemed to make them crave living intensely. Things that would pass in a blink for those who lived for centuries were *urgent* to mortals. It was beautiful.

As Carissa and Sionnach walked toward the tiny diner he liked, he offered her his arm. He tried to move slower with her, careful in his movements so he didn't slip and reveal his Otherness. *Technically,* a faery shouldn't ever reveal his true nature to a mortal. Exceptions were only to be made in extreme circumstances—a detail Sionnach used to justify giving so much information to Jayce. Sionnach considered the well-being and safety of the desert just such a circumstance; he simply hadn't quite verbalized how Jayce fit into his plans before allowing the mortal boy such rare access. Rika's anger over Sionnach's lies of omission made sense, but once she calmed down, she'd see that his plan had been the only solution left to him at that moment.

She has to.

As Carissa snuggled close to Sionnach, he pushed his anxieties away to focus on her. "I've missed you lately," he told her.

"I worried that you were"—she blushed—"bored with me."

"For some reason, I don't find you at all boring." He rubbed his cheek against her hair, before nuzzling his face against her throat to smell her. Then he kissed her neck, partly so she didn't notice that he enjoyed sniffing her.

She giggled.

"I like you," he said simply. "I missed you, but it wasn't a good time to see you. I had things I needed to deal with."

Then, before she could ask questions he couldn't answer

honestly, he gave her a proper kiss. She looked dazed when he pulled back.

"Okay," she whispered.

He grinned at her before opening the door of the diner. "After you, lovely . . ."

Sionnach learned years ago that mortals appreciated it when his manners were theater-elegant. She might not be in pearls and velvet, but she was beautiful and should be treated like it. He tucked her hand into the crook of his arm and was rewarded with another adoring look.

A few steps in, she stopped and said, "You realize that we're at a total *dive,* right?"

He looked around with feigned shock. "This? My staff tells me this is a prime establishment."

He led her to a booth and brushed crumbs to the floor. The seat had a visible gash in it, and the tabletop was carved with former patrons' names. The table tilted just a bit as he put a hand on it. But, like so many places in the desert, there was a defiance in the beauty of the old diner that glimmered just under the surface.

"Your seat, my dear."

She slid into the booth and looked up at him curiously.

He ducked his head in a flare of instinctive shyness—fearing that he was wrong about her, worrying that she would hate it—and looked up at her through the hair that fell over his eyes. "Is it too awful for you?"

"No." She reached out and caught his wrist, tugging him until he sat beside her. "I'm with you, so it's *perfect.*"

Somewhat embarrassed, he admitted, "My finances are lacking."

She entwined her fingers with his. "Don't worry about it. There's no real jobs here . . . or places to go or . . ." She looked out the window at the partially lit signs, scrubby plants, and cracked asphalt. "This whole place is awful. As soon as I can, I'm out of here."

Sionnach tensed. He wasn't surprised at the vehement tone in her voice, but he didn't see the world the same way she did. He wanted her to see it as he did, to maybe stay here a while longer. "It can be wonderful here too. Beautiful. There are treasures here that I haven't found anywhere else . . . and we have fun, don't we?"

She turned to smile at him. "It's not awful with *you* here, but it was before."

As Carissa snuggled into Sionnach's embrace, he glanced down at their entwined fingers. She might be a mortal, but he'd miss her. If he were a mortal, he'd follow her for a time to whatever place she fled to, but he wasn't. He wouldn't ever be. The desert was always going to be his rightful place, and she was—like all mortals—a lovely distraction and fleeting moment in his eternity.

Outside the window, four solitary faeries rushed up and pressed their faces to the glass. They were his responsibility, but he'd told them previously that they weren't to intrude when he was with human girls. Although Carissa couldn't see them, she obviously felt him tense beside her because she asked, "Are you okay?"

"How could I be anything else? I'm with you," he assured her. He hadn't actually answered the question, but overt lies were impossible. Luckily, like most people, Carissa didn't notice simple misdirection.

When she looked away, scanning the room for their server, Sionnach scowled at the faeries. He subtly tilted his head upward in a gesture that clearly conveyed that they should depart. Instead of obeying, they mocked him—one swept another into an exaggerated dip, a second folded his hands and clutched them over his heart with a moony expression. They weren't doing anything horrible, but he didn't want an audience. He didn't want them to bring their reminders of his responsibilities and challenges into his rare time at pretending to be free.

"Go away," he mouthed silently.

Carissa glanced at him. "Are you sure you're okay?"

He smiled reassuringly before he said, "I was merely thinking."

"About?"

"Well . . ." He leaned in close to her as if he were going to say something serious and then whispered, "*Food.*"

Carissa laughed.

A waitress dropped a menu on the table with a *thunk.*

"How almost kind!" Sionnach gave her an irritated look and lifted one of the sticky menus to hold it out to Carissa. As he reached for the other menu, he saw that his disobedient faeries had donned mortal glamours and were walking into the restaurant. Gone were their tails and thorns. Instead, they now looked like standard desert-living teens. Their clothes were all a little worn, but their overall appearance was that of a rowdy group of potential troublemakers rather than absurdly long-living creatures who needed to be kept in check by their Alpha. It wasn't that they were *bad* in the mortal sense of right and wrong; faeries were merely less cautious, more mischievous, and often unmindful of the breakable nature of more finite creatures.

Sionnach didn't want to deal with their testing of his rules—not here, not in front of her—but they came up to the booth. One dragged a chair over to the booth. Two others slid into the bench facing Sionnach and Carissa. The fourth stayed standing.

"Shy?" Carissa looked at them warily.

"It's fine." He kept an arm around her.

The waitress, who had been watching them with a pronounced scowl, headed back over to the table. She stopped just behind the standing faery and announced, "No orders, no seats." She paused and glared at Sionnach before adding, "Your friends need to order or get out."

"They aren't staying." He looked at them one by one, hoping that they'd walk away.

They grinned unrepentantly.

"We could order food," one said.

"And pay for it," the waitresses said sternly.

"Sure," another faery replied.

"No." Sionnach gave them a look that was more bared teeth than actual smile, warning them that they were treading on shaky ground. "You need to leave."

The faery on the chair asked, "Where's Rika? I didn't see her around. Did she go back with Keenan?"

"Who?" Carissa tensed and started to pull out of Sionnach's embrace.

"Tsk. Tsk. You didn't tell her about Rika?"

"Rika is my family," Sionnach murmured to Carissa as the faeries flashed mock innocent looks. Then, his gaze still on the faeries: "She'll be home soon, and she would *not* like you attempting to stir trouble in her absence."

Carissa started, "Your family? Is she your sister or—"

"My family . . . more or less adopted her. It's like she was born one of us now."

"Oh." Carissa sounded relieved, and then instantly a little hurt. "Why haven't I met her? Or heard about her? You've never even mentioned her."

"What terrible manners!" the faery standing beside the table said with a gasp. "Carissa, darling, you ought to come with us instead."

At that, Sionnach's patience expired. He stood in a move almost too quick for mortal eyes. The faery who was standing and the one who'd dragged the chair over both jumped and promptly scurried backward. Calmly, Sionnach said, "Carissa, would you go up to the counter and ask our waitress for a piece of pie?"

"Sure." She stretched the word out. "And how long do you need me gone in search of this pie?"

Sionnach flashed her a toothy smile. That was part of her

charm: she didn't ask questions he couldn't answer or expect him to behave like he was completely civilized. "Just a few minutes," he assured her. "Your patience is kind, Riss."

"In case your lips are bruised later . . ." She slid out of the booth and kissed him full on the mouth.

He wrapped his arms around her and lifted her while they kissed. When he pulled away, he turned and lowered her feet; in the process, he moved her away from the other faeries. "Never too bruised for you," he whispered. "Go on now."

She walked away laughing with a swish in her steps. Unlike Rika, Carissa didn't question him when he asserted his dominance. If anything, she seemed excited when she glimpsed it.

As soon as she was at the counter, her back to them, Sionnach turned to face the faeries. His words were low as he ordered, "Leave. Now."

The faery who had remained standing was suddenly very serious. "There is taking of sides. There are words, Sionnach. There are rumors that Maili has invited Keenan to—"

"He is not welcome in my desert." Sionnach pulled his shoulders back. His tail—which the faeries could see although mortals, fortunately, could not—was held high and to the side in an aggressive posture. He flashed his teeth.

One of the seated faeries stood and raised a hand as if he'd strike Sionnach. "Maybe it's not *your* desert after all."

Sionnach punched him, an uppercut to the face. "You forget yourself."

The waitress called out, "Fights *outside*. Not in here."

"There is no fight," Sionnach answered without taking his attention from the faery staring at him. *"Is there?"*

"If you can't keep us safe, maybe there *should* be," the faery said.

"Do you challenge me?"

Several heartbeats passed as they all waited.

The faery looked down and took a step back. "No. Not me."

The other faeries didn't move, but they all lowered their gazes to the ground submissively.

The one faery who had remained seated stood finally. Like Sionnach, he was a fox, but his tail was tucked between his legs. Quietly, he said, "Rika ran because *Keenan*'s coming here. The Summer King. *Here!*" He looked around worriedly, lowered his voice further still, and said, "He'll change everything. Even *Rika* is afraid. She left because—"

"Rika didn't run from Keenan." Sionnach felt a wash of exhaustion. He'd hoped that no one had noticed her absence, figured that with the way she hid in her cave they'd assume she was tucked away, but she'd obviously been seen. Gently, he said, "I'm sure she'll be back."

From beside him, the faery with the bruised face prompted, "And the rest?"

"We'll fix it. Rika intends to . . . *talk* to Maili." Sionnach's tail swished behind him. "And if you are wise, you'll want seats to watch. Rika is not pleased that Maili invited Keenan into our desert. He has no right being near her ever again. We will not allow him here, and we *will* keep you safe."

"But—"

"Have I failed you yet?" Sionnach looked at each of them in turn.

"No," several said simultaneously.

"I told you I'd find a way to have Rika help me keep you safe. I *did*." Sionnach let them see his affection for them for a moment.

"Rika will come back?" the twitchy faery asked.

"This is her home," he said. Hoping they didn't notice that he'd avoided the question, he quickly added, "If I fail you, you have every right to anger, but I will *not* fail. I have not."

"Rika will stand beside you? Keep him out?" the fox faery asked nervously. "I like it here, but I don't want a king. Kings aren't . . . good. We're solitary and—"

"I will keep us all safe," Sionnach interrupted him. "I always do. Trust me."

After a quiet moment, all four faeries left. Sionnach let out a whoosh of breath. He needed Rika to come back, to forgive him or at least ignore her anger to look after the solitaries here. He was mostly certain she would return, but a niggling doubt remained. She'd held on to her anger at Keenan for decades. Grudge holding was something of an art for her. *This*, he rationalized, *wasn't a major offense though. Surely she could see that! A harmless omission, a few nudges toward what she already wanted, and some gentle manipulation* . . . Among fey, these weren't even worth noticing. He'd give her the day, and after that, he'd have to find her. If she wanted to rage at him later, she could, but right now, they had the safety of the desert to consider.

Matter resolved, Sionnach sat down and looked toward the mortal girl he'd grown to like.

Carissa walked back toward the table, accompanied by the waitress, who was carrying a slice of pie. Carissa slid back into the booth and snuggled up to him again.

The waitress smiled approving at Sionnach as she set the pie down in front of him. "Good riddance to them. That lot always starts trouble in here."

"I'll speak to them about that." Sionnach flashed her a quicksilver grin and then ordered a glass of milk for himself, as well as a burger, fries, and a soda for Carissa.

After the waitress walked away, Carissa was quiet for a minute before she asked, "Who's Keenan?"

"Rika's ex . . ." Sionnach felt weary. "He wasn't kind to her, and it's taken her years to even think about trusting again."

Carissa squeezed his hand. "Will she be okay?"

"Yes," Sionnach vowed. "We'll find a way to keep her free of him. Everyone will be fine. It's just a matter of finding ways to make it so."

Carissa leaned against him. "You're a good person."

"No, not usually," Sionnach admitted. "But I do try to protect my own."

* * *

A few hours later, Sionnach stood waiting for Carissa to meet him in the ghost town where he'd been sleeping of late. They'd separated after their meal, her to run an errand and him to take some time with the sand and sun to think. He liked that he didn't have to tell her that he couldn't ride inside her vehicle, that such machines made him sick. They'd been spending enough time together of late that she didn't ask questions when he made decisions that might otherwise seem peculiar. That, too, was a benefit of living in the desert. Out here, the sense of what was "normal" was wide and varied. Desert towns were the safe havens of mortals who didn't want to be trapped by society—and faeries who weren't willing to be a part of the courts. Peculiar was the norm here.

This ghost town had once been the only outpost in this part of the desert. It stood here when he first realized that Rika was living in a nearby cave. Back then, Silver Ridge was filled with mortals. Much like the ones living in the new desert town, those long-gone mortals were a mix of adventurers and lost souls. Some came to make a new life; others came to hide. They were all dead now, had been for decades. The town was dead too. It had been abandoned, and aside from the occasional photographer or hiker, the ghost town was Sionnach's very own space, his personal hideaway and one of his regular resting spots.

Some of the buildings were standing, but others were shells now. He liked it that way, with saloon doors standing in a frame with no walls to support them. Behind those doors was a sheer drop to a ravine. When the ground had crumbled, he'd always thought that there was something strangely poetic about the still-standing doors. The town was clustered along a street, but on the hill stood an abandoned mining shack and a partial bit of track, broken but still present.

Sionnach watched Carissa pull up in her faded red Jeep. Although she turned off the engine, she didn't get out of the vehicle. Before he'd met her, Sionnach had seen her out here with a group of people, drinking and dancing under the full desert moon. He liked the sense of freedom she reveled in that night, but he also appreciated the cautious way she looked around today.

He stayed invisible to her eyes until he reached one of the reasonably intact saloon-style buildings. Then, he turned to face her and became visible so it appeared as if he had just exited the building. He walked over the broken wood of the building's porch toward the front railing with the sort of grace he knew she admired. An older mortal might find his foxlike agility peculiar, but Carissa didn't question how or why he could move so quickly.

Carissa hopped out of the vehicle, watching him silently.

He knew better than to relax his rules too much, but he liked the intense way she studied him. He preened a bit under her attention, not quite revealing his Otherness, but not playing mortal as much as he typically would either. He allowed himself to be too sinuous as he leaped over the rail, too fast as he came to stand beside her in a bit of a blur, too different to truly be thought mortal.

She was wide-eyed and enthralled. "How did you—"

"Hello." He took both of her hands in his, using them to pull her toward him—and away from the metal of the vehicle. Still holding her hands, he tugged her close enough to kiss. Some faeries were addictive to mortals; fox faeries weren't. The only danger to her from his kisses would be if he were unscrupulous, and although he was far from honest with the mortals he wooed, he didn't take advantage of them. He didn't even sanction lying with them; the risk of fathering half-fey children was too great. So, he kissed her until she was breathless, and then he pulled away.

For the rest of the day, they explored the buildings. They picnicked on a brightly colored blanket with bold lines that he kept here for just this reason. His objective was to show Carissa the beauty of the desert, to let her see it as he did. He found a beautiful Mojave rattlesnake, interesting rocks, and Joshua trees. He pointed out the tip of a cougar's tail on an outcropping, watching it vanish. He knew she would leave in the next few months, and—selfishly perhaps—he wanted her to remember him, to think of the desert as he knew it.

When evening fell, Sionnach walked Carissa back to her Jeep. Above them, the sky seemed to go on forever, and the distant sight of the cliffs and cacti in the dusk was gorgeous. Heat shimmered close to the earth as the warmth in the ground and the cool air of evening connected. Usually, he would be happy to be in the desert on his own, but tonight he wanted someone to share it with; he wanted the sort of union that he'd never had—one he couldn't have until he was able to be with his true mate. He wouldn't have relations with a mortal, but a night spent kissing and touching under the stars was tempting. In some quiet part of his mind, he could admit that Carissa would only be standing in for the one he wanted, but tonight, he simply didn't want to be alone. In a moment of weakness, he blurted out, "I'm camping out here tonight. Maybe you could stay."

She paused, kissed him, and said, "Well, if we were inside one of the buildings . . . I mean snakes wouldn't get into the sleeping bag, right?"

"You'd stay? Really?" He pulled her into his arms again, torn between guilt and hopefulness. "With me?"

She laughed, not coquettishly but as if surprised. He had been the one keeping their kisses tame; he had been the one not pushing the lines.

"In a heartbeat . . . but . . ." She glanced at her watch. "I'm already going to be late." She bit her lip, and then after a moment, she offered, "I could call my father on the way home tomorrow and say I had a flat or something."

Sionnach brushed her hair from her face. He knew better than this. He was the Alpha here, the one tasked with setting the rules that the other solitaries followed. "But?"

"I'll be grounded probably."

"And they'd worry all night. . . ." He rested his forehead against hers. "Waking up with you beside me would be beautiful, but I don't think either of us is ready for the costs of that."

"Either of us?"

He pulled back to stare into her face and half answered her question: "I like seeing you. If you're grounded . . ."

"Oh." She blushed and ducked her head. "*That* cost. I thought you meant there was something else wrong."

Faeries don't keep mortals, he thought quietly to himself. *What would you say if you saw what I am? What if things went too far and there were a child?* That thought reinforced his resolve. Half-fey children were dangerous to birth, and the courts stole them away if they were discovered. He wouldn't wish injury to Carissa or cope with the loss of any child of his. He smiled at her and opened the door of her car. "Go home, Carissa, before my morals flee again."

She climbed into the Jeep, and Sionnach hid his hand behind his back so she couldn't see that touching the steel of the door bruised it. He kissed her lightly and stepped away.

"See you soon?" Carissa asked hopefully.

"As soon as possible."

She nodded and drove away into the desert, leaving him to ponder his weaknesses.

Chapter 19

Donia invited Rika and her mortal into the least formal of the sitting rooms. She suspected that the last Winter Queen had intended to have this room renovated, but the shabbiness of it was oddly comfortable. The rug that covered the hardwood floor was almost threadbare, although the muted greens and golds still somehow seemed opulent. More than once, Donia had thought that the rug was more suited to a museum than daily use. Delicate snow globes lined a shelf on the wall, proof perhaps that the dead queen had possessed a sense of humor. The only vibrant thing in the room was the bright crimson chair where Donia now sat with her bare feet curled under her. The rest of the furnishings were all muted with age, reminding her of the cottage where she'd lived when she was the Winter Girl. She felt like this room wasn't as tainted by her predecessor's often disquieting taste. The rest of the house she'd been slowly changing, but here she felt at peace.

Rika's mortal, Jayce, sat on a faded floral divan. Rika, however, was pacing angrily as she said, "Keenan is trying to force allegiances."

"With your solitary desert faeries?"

"Yes!"

"Which is unacceptable," Donia said.

"I can't let him force the desert under his control." Rika paused in the middle of the rug and caught Donia's gaze. "*I* won't be under his control, not again, not ever again."

Donia remained motionless. "I see."

"The Summer King is too focused on strengthening his court."

"That hasn't changed." Absently, Donia smoothed her skirt over her ankles, thinking about the long-gone days when she'd needed boots in the cold winter. Now, the cold radiated from her very skin, and footwear was a nuisance.

"It *won't* change, and others will continue to pay the price. Maybe not like we did, but it's still all about him." Rika folded her arms over her chest.

Donia knew that the price they both had paid for Keenan's single-sighted attention to his goals was high, but it appeared that they were both again being caught in the machinations of the Summer King. It was his actions that had led to Donia's being made queen—trying to remake a court that had thrived on violence and unchecked power for centuries. Ruling wasn't without its benefits, but it was not the freedom she'd dreamed of one day having, nor was it a union with the only faery she'd ever loved. No, in his pursuit of his queen, Donia had been left injured. Her choices had been death or becoming the embodiment of Winter, and with it, being unable to touch the Summer King without pain to them both.

"Now that he's stronger, I need help," Rika said, drawing Donia out of her reverie. "He's working with solitaries who shouldn't have power. They are vile to mortals. One stabbed the desert Alpha, Sionnach. . . ."

"And you?"

"I can hold order against even the strongest solitaries. I've just not been interested"—Rika glanced at Jayce—"but things change. I'm willing to keep order, with or without the current Alpha, but I need something—*someone*—to spare me from Keenan's meddling. I need a regent who will allow me to keep most of my autonomy. . . ."

Donia nodded. "You want me as a buffer between you and Keenan."

Rika dropped to her knees on the rug in front of Donia. "I would offer you my fealty. I would be your subject—not his. *Never* his."

"Pledging your support would mean fighting should I ask it of you. It could mean moving or surrendering anything I ask of you—" Donia glanced meaningfully at Jayce.

At that, Jayce said, "I'll offer you my loyalty too if you accept a human's fealty."

Donia smiled at his unexpected offer, and a shower of ice crystals like falling stars appeared in the air. "Mortals don't generally pledge to a court, as they don't even know we exist, but I'd offer you my court's protection if you love my sister enough."

Jayce knelt beside Rika and took her hand in his. "Done."

Rika bowed her head and vowed, "I vow to obey you, Donia. I will fight at your word, hold your friends as my own, and your enemies as my own."

Jayce echoed her words.

"Your vow"—Donia reached a hand out to touch Rika and Jayce's entwined hands—"is accepted. The Winter Court proclaims you *both* as our own."

"Not just sister, but Queen," Rika whispered. Then with a small smile, she came to her feet and embraced Donia.

And Donia tried not to think of what Keenan's reaction would be when he learned what she had done. There weren't many times that she had stood against him yet. It was the nature of their courts to be in opposition, but hers was still so much stronger that she had no need yet to be cruel. This, though, he would see as an insult. She sent a messenger to tell his faeries what she'd done, to invite the inevitable conversation to happen in her territory.

Hours later, they had moved to the Winter Garden to await Keenan's arrival. Donia knew he'd come soon, and she'd rather not destroy the house with the inevitable argument that would accompany his appearance. She was more comfortable out here in the frost-heavy grass. It was one of the spots where she came for solace now. Inside, there were faeries awaiting her orders, seeking favors, or trying to make sense of their new queen. In the garden, there was silence. Wooden benches—fitted together by a craftsman's skill, no screws or bolts anywhere in them—were tucked among the trees and shrubbery. Bird feeders and winter plants invited animals to find nourishment, and a few tamed creatures crept from their dens to seek her company. Beside the bench slept one such creature, an arctic fox. Only its dark eyes and nose showed in the snow bank. The rest of its body blended with the stark white ground. Absently, Donia ran her bare toes over its back.

Rika and Jayce were cuddled together on another bench. They had heaps of furs wrapped around them like blankets, and Donia smiled at the way Rika stroked the pelt across her lap. It was good to see her less angry at the past she'd known. For years as the Winter Girl, these same furs were what they'd had for blankets. When Rika had been freed, she'd cast off most everything that reminded her of the life she'd been living. When Donia became the Winter Girl, she hadn't realized the extent of Rika's anger. Over time, she'd seen through the illusion that Rika had created to protect Donia. Rika had been far more furious than she'd admitted. Once Donia realized that, Rika stopped visiting, as if she couldn't bear to see reminders of the curse. Now, though, Rika finally seemed closer to *actual* peace. Her time in the desert had mellowed her—perhaps her mortal had helped too.

A red-eyed Hawthorn Girl alit from the tree branches; her wings glittered as if the frost clung to her. "The Summer King is here."

"Let the games begin," Donia murmured.

Rika reached for Jayce's hand.

Donia smiled. "Rika?"

She looked up at her queen, a question plain in her eyes.

"Nothing has changed . . . not truly. I won't silence your voice," Donia said. "I owe you too much for that."

The look Rika gave her was one of extreme gratitude and relief. Some of the tension left her body. "You are kinder than I could ever be."

Keenan strode into the garden, glowing brightly enough that Rika darted forward to shield Jayce with her body. "Turn off the glow. There's a mortal here."

The light blinked out, but the heat was still oppressive. The garden was in a fast melt. Water poured from the trees where ice had covered the branches a heartbeat before—it looked like a waterfall crashing to the ground and rushing away.

Two of the Hawthorn Girls pulled Jayce toward the house in a flash of movement. By the time Keenan stood staring at Donia, Jayce was safely out of reach. Rika felt foolish for even bringing him, but now wasn't the time for such thoughts.

"What have you done?" Keenan snapped. Earth was boiling at his feet, bubbling up in black ooze.

"It's good to see you too." Donia pointedly lowered one bare foot to the earth, holding her skirt up just a bit so her bare ankles and calves were visible. Snow spread from her foot over the earth in a thickening blanket.

"Don . . ." He raked a hand through his hair. "*Why?*"

"She came offering fealty." Donia was motionless, winter-still. The only movement was the ice and snow crackling out over the ground. Water droplets froze mid-fall, forming icy spires under the tree, sharp, jutting angles that looked menacing in direct contrast to the calm on her face and in her tone. "This is a Winter Court matter, between a queen and her subjects."

"You *know* . . ." He growled in frustration. "She told you I offered her my protect—"

"I refused. Several times," Rika interrupted. She shivered in the icy blast of Donia's temper.

Keenan ignored Rika.

"She's a desert-dweller," he said.

"Strong enough to be Alpha, as I understand."

"You can't even walk there, Donia. Even at the height of the last Winter Queen's power, she couldn't take the desert." Steam sizzled around him as the snow approached him like a white wave. It melted as fast as it grew. The ice didn't recede from the garden, but the area around him had become verdant. Plants were flowering at his feet, and a morning glory vine was twined around his leg, blossoming.

"I don't want to *rule* it, Keenan, but allies . . . perhaps it's good to have allies, especially when Summer is trying my patience." Donia schooled her features to keep her less regal emotions hidden. He was beautiful, and the anger on him only heightened that. This wasn't the time for such thoughts. She would let Rika have her words with Keenan, and then . . . then Donia would enjoy the sight of the Summer King.

* * *

As the two regents exchanged words, one of the Winter fey reached for Rika, but she wasn't done yet. She'd brought this problem to Donia's court, sought intervention, but all three knew that Keenan's actions were what had pushed her into needing to do so. He wouldn't be returning to the desert now, and although she was grateful that she'd not see him again, she wanted to say her piece before leaving.

"You pushed me," she said, interrupting the silence between Keenan and Donia. "You made the mistake of thinking I was yours to manipulate. . . ."

"So you swore loyalty to my *opposing* court? I offered to protect you, to strengthen the safety of the desert, and you do *this*?" Keenan's voice made clear that his emotions were riding high.

"It would be neutral territory if you hadn't tried to bully me," Rika told him.

He stared at her with hurt plain on his face. Once that hurt would've made her agree to anything he asked. Now she held his gaze unflinchingly.

Air so hot that it was hazy beat against her as he stalked forward. The greenery around his feet extended with him. The Summer King unbound and angry was a daunting thing, and Rika had a brief moment of gratitude that he hadn't been so forceful when he'd visited her in the desert a few weeks ago.

Sweat formed on Rika's face, but she stood her ground.

A tree branch overhead burst into bloom so forcefully that the ice launched from it like an explosion. He looked sad, as if the shattering of ice had transformed his temper into sorrow. His volatility hadn't decreased with his being unbound. If anything, in this moment, she would say that it had grown worse. Back when she was a girl he was trying to woo, she hadn't seen his moods. Then, she saw only the charm. Later, when she tried to convince girl after girl not to trust him, she'd seen his temper and his sorrow. Even then, his sorrow worked on her more than his anger ever would.

He stopped in front of her, his eyes filled with loss and longing, and said, "I am not your enemy, Rika."

Unwilling to let him have even a moment of victory, Rika pointed out, "You are not my friend either. You never were. You were my almost lover, my biggest mistake, my opposition, but you were never my friend. Friends don't turn away when someone is lost and hurt, when someone is *freezing . . . literally freezing* for trusting the wrong person."

Behind her, she knew Donia waited, the cool flow of arctic air pushing forward, easing the unpleasant sting of heat, and Rika was surprised to find the cold momentarily comforting.

Keenan opened his mouth, but before he could utter a misdirection or perhaps an apology, she said, "The fey in the desert have their freedom now even though it cost me mine. That is the choice I made. This time I chose to sacrifice my freedom knowingly, not as a result of lies."

"Faeries can't l—"

"Shading the truth is the same as lying, Keenan. Failing

to tell dozens of girls what they are truly risking is the worst kind of lie." She felt tears on her cheeks. "Don't pretend that faeries are truthful. I *am* one now. I know exactly what we are capable of doing."

For a moment he said nothing, and she had a sliver of softening in her anger. Then he spoke. "You rage that the ice was so horrific that you retreated to the desert for *years*, yet you chose Donia's court. Wouldn't you rather have the sunlight? We can work this out. Offer your fealty to me instead. . . ."

Even now, he focused only on what he wanted. She shouldn't be surprised, not really. She'd said for years that he'd never change. Rika looked over her shoulder to see Donia. The Winter Queen didn't look worried. She knew Rika too well to think that Keenan's words would convince her.

"Keenan," Rika started.

He reached for her wrist.

"No." She pulled her hand to her stomach to avoid his touch, and then flung it forward and up to strike his face.

Keenan captured her fist in his hand and kissed her knuckles. "You've made a bad choice."

This time the Winter Queen *did* speak. "Don't touch her again."

The possessive anger in Donia's voice made Rika grateful that the Winter Queen knew that Rika no longer loved the flirtatious Summer King. He was not made for constancy; his court was one of frolicking, not faithfulness. When Rika had been forced to spend decades in his company watching him woo mortal after mortal, knowing that he spoke words of forever to them as he once had to her, she'd hated him. She'd hated herself more for having once believed that he meant those pretty promises. Since then, she'd thought that he could not mean them, had never meant them, but as Keenan's gaze fell on Donia, Rika realized that she'd been wrong. Every beautiful dream Keenan had ever whispered was true—just not for the hundreds of girls before Donia. The Summer King truly loved the Winter Queen.

Rika would never tell him, but if he would have still smiled at her that way when she had been filled with ice—*or even last year*, she reluctantly admitted to herself—she would've said yes to most any question he asked. There were very few things in the world as beautiful as the Summer King's smile when he was in love. Even still, Rika wished she could save Donia from the hurt of being loved by Keenan. Unfortunately, she'd been unable to do that when Donia was a mortal, and she certainly couldn't do it now.

"I'm sorry, Donia," she whispered. "I'm so very sorry I couldn't protect you from this life."

In a blink, Donia was standing behind her, gently squeezing her hand in acknowledgment of those whispered words.

"Go home, Rika," her queen said evenly. Her gaze was still fastened on Keenan, and it was very clear that she still loved the Summer King, despite being cursed to be Winter

Girl and now being the regent of his opposing court. Without looking away from Keenan, the Winter Queen added, "If you need anything, my court—and my allies who *can* enter the desert to aid you—will be here to call upon."

Silently, Rika walked toward the house. The door opened at her approach, and another Hawthorn Girl stepped aside to let her pass.

From the relative shelter of the doorway, Rika glanced back to see Keenan brush his hand over Donia's hair. At his touch, the Winter Queen's hair became soft blond instead of ice-white. She leaned into his caress for a heartbeat, face flushed and steam rising from her skin. He was no better off: ice clung to his hair, his fingertips, and his lips. The curse had been cruelest to these two. Despite not being the Summer Queen he'd sought, Donia was someone he loved. Rika's heart hurt for both of them when she realized that, despite everything, the two regents were in love—and no more likely to find a future than they had been when she'd been first cursed.

Donia stayed still until Rika was gone. She knew well that her court would relax now that the former Winter Girl and her mortal were safely away. The stakes in her quarrels with Keenan had always been high, and not too many decades ago, faeries had died when her temper was left unchecked. No one save another regent could survive if they were caught between Summer and Winter in true conflict—and Donia wasn't sure how angry the Summer King was.

"The desert wasn't yours to take," Keenan said. His hand was next to her face, not touching, but near enough that his hand almost caressed Donia's cheek. She'd settled for these half touches for so long, dreamed they could be more, and then he'd found his queen.

And I am an afterthought yet again.

She turned and kissed the palm of his hand; as she did so, her hair brushed against his arm, and even that brief caress left frost-flowers traced on his skin. "You're wrong. It's *all* mine to take, Keenan . . . especially if it brings you to my step."

The sky grew gray, and a fierce shriek from a sudden storm gave voice to the hurt Donia couldn't. The air became snow-filled. Still, glowing at the center was Keenan, illuminated in sunlight, still smiling at the faery who stood against him. All around him was a blizzard, but he looked happy.

He'd broken her heart time and again, but all Donia could think was that he was here and he was hers in this instant. *Not Rika's. Not Ash's. Not any of the former Winter Girls or current Summer Girls.* He smiled, and she shoved a torrent of ice at him. His answering flare of sunlight turned every bit of ice into steam.

She knew that her court was inside the safety of her home and would turn their faces away. Like her, they too often looked on him with affection. Centuries ago, he'd been a child who'd played in this Winter Garden, the son of another queen, a queen he'd killed. The woman who'd cursed him and her both had bid them to cherish him, and they still did.

"I miss you," he whispered into the storm.

"Yet you curl up with your queen and leave me alone," she reminded him.

"Don—"

"No," she interrupted. "I know every objection, every word, every wish you'll utter, Keenan. I've heard them for decades."

"You *know* I never wanted this," he swore. His sunlit skin glowed as he walked toward her, stalking her like she was something he could capture.

Embarrassingly, she wanted to be captured.

When she stayed still, letting the ice roll out across the ground but not striking him, he paused. His eyes widened slightly. "Don?"

"This doesn't mean I forgive you," she whispered, and then she pulled him to her, unmindful of the burns his sunlight left on her skin and the frostbite she left on his. They'd obliterate each other one day if they kept this up, but she couldn't step away any more than he could.

This is who we are. This is how we destroy everything. He'd turned away from her, abandoned her for his Summer Queen. Even now that he was back, he was trying his damnedest to convince his queen to accept him. *Aislinn is his queen; he should be with her.* Donia understood everything he'd done—why he'd rejected her, why he'd tried to romance his queen. She could even admit that she might've done the same things in his position. *We're wrong together.* He was the embodiment of Summer, and she was Winter. Everything about them was in opposition.

This will end badly.

But when he kissed her it was hard to remember why it was so wrong, and when she pressed her body to his, she couldn't help but wonder if the cost was worth it.

Chapter 20

Sionnach sat atop the roof of one of the dilapidated buildings. Beneath him a broken door hung crookedly in the frame. A few years ago, Sionnach had replaced the hinges, but he wasn't a carpenter, so it sagged oddly. On either side of the door was a window frame. One had dirty glass with a spiderweb crack running through it. The other frame was open; no glass remained where the window should be.

Across from him were the remains of other buildings, and over top that the sky was a riot of colors as the sun rose. Below him he could see the faeries who were walking through the deserted streets, clustering in groups on the porches, sitting in window frames, perched on other railings. None were brazen enough to climb up as high as he was. His position was a statement, and they knew it.

The view from the roof of this building was among the best, and the view of him was imposing. Part of being Alpha was simply a game: show the others that he was the most daunting faery here. He wasn't, hadn't been so since Rika had arrived in the desert, but she'd disdained anything that had a taint of the political to it. He couldn't blame her, not really. The Summer King and the now-dead Winter Queen had both done their level best to destroy her. It wasn't personal; she was just one of the many pawns in their conflict.

Sionnach ignored the faeries milling about, instead studying the dusty streets and scrubby plants that grew alongside sagging porches and storefronts. One porch had a dry-rotted plank, but after the first faery stepped on it and put his foot through the wood, the others realized not to step there.

For now, he didn't move from his position. He didn't glance at them, even though they were staring at him. Some were openly curious, but still he waited, letting the tension build.

Finally, a faery who was leaning against a railing kitty-corner from the building he was on called out, "Sionnach?"

He let his gaze drop to the crowd of faeries, taking their measure, dragging it out to keep the tension high. "Well then . . ." he drawled. "Are we having a party I didn't know about?"

A few faeries smiled, but no one answered. Instead, there was a restless shifting around, foot shuffling, and downcast gazes. They were nervous. Maili had caused that, sowing seeds of dissention and inviting the Summer King to walk among them. There were reasons they all eschewed the courts; more than a few solitaries had once belonged in one or another court—not all of the solitaries, of course, but at least a few of their number had lived among the stiffer sort of faeries. Some had left on their own; others had been cast out. A few had even lived in Faerie itself, a place ruled by an unchanging queen who—if myths were true—was one of the first fey. Here in the desert was as far from Faerie and the courts as they could get.

And Maili would have a regent come here!

Sionnach remained as still as when he was watching the sky; his expression didn't hint at his thoughts or his feelings about the assembled faeries' scrutiny. His jacket was folded over one leg, and his posture was relaxed. Almost casually, he looked up at the sun. "I've been here far too long to want to move. Things don't often change out here . . . not really. But sometimes, changes *must* happen."

They waited.

"We need to work on letting the mortals have peace here."

Grumbling rose up at Sionnach's words.

"Why?"

"Where's the sport in *that*?"

"Just because you're with—"

Sionnach fixed the latter faery with a glare that stopped him mid-sentence. Then, he looked back out at the sky and said, "The new Winter Queen was once a mortal. The missing Summer Queen was a mortal. The new Dark King loved a mortal. Would you have any of the courts come here angry?" He looked at them, allowing his gaze to slowly drift over the crowd, before adding, "Or would you keep your freedom?"

A few nodded. Some exchanged looks with one another. They knew; they mightn't like it, but they knew that he was right. All things changed in time. As mortals spread over the world, mingling more and more in the matters of faeries, a change was upon them all. Maybe if the courts had never left Faerie things would be different, but they had left. They'd come here, set up their courts and lived among mortals. Now, because of a curse, mortals had become fey, and as the regents loved and lived with mortals, their stances had changed. Sionnach had to do his part to protect those under his sway in the desert.

"I won't let Maili or her ilk take away my right as Alpha in our home." Sionnach bared his teeth. "Aside from Rika, no one here is strong enough to wrest power from me."

"And where *is* Rika?" a faery asked.

Sionnach didn't even glance his way, much less answer the question. "You will all follow the new rules or pay the price."

A faery with a wicked grin said, "Why? I *heard* you were too injured to—"

At that Sionnach was off the roof and in a fraction of a moment had knocked the faery to the sand. The jacket from Sionnach's lap dropped to the ground in the process.

As Sionnach pressed his arm to the faery's throat, he looked over his shoulder at the crowd standing around them in a loose circle now. "I'm feeling quite fine. Good of you to ask. . . ."

The faery grasped at the sand near him, searching for a weapon and finding a piece of broken wood nearby. His fingertips grazed it, and almost immediately, he gripped it and swung.

Seemingly without looking, Sionnach caught the faery's wrist and forced it to the ground. Then, he looked into the faery's face and whispered, "Don't."

The faery nodded and released the weapon. As soon as he did so, Sionnach let go of him and stood. The faery scrabbled backward and sat so that he was leaning against a building.

"Follow the rules or move on." Sionnach brushed the sand and dirt off his hands and knees, using the gesture to buy himself time to will away the pain that the moment of conflict had caused. Schooling his features into an approximation of a smile, he stood and looked around at them before adding, "We aren't a court here. You can obey or move on. Your choice. But it might be good to remember that Rika supports my decision. She's not hiding away in her cave anymore, and she is never going to be weak enough for any of you to defeat."

Several faeries exchanged looks, as if they were debating trying Sionnach.

"I am the Alpha in this desert." Sionnach kept his spine straight, still hiding the pain that was now flooding him, and doing his best to look unconcerned about another potential altercation. "Don't doubt that."

Then he bent down, grabbed his jacket from the ground, and slipped it on. "Obey the new rules if you mean to stay here."

He tucked his hands in the jacket pockets and pulled the jacket closed before he walked through the crowd and away into the desert, consciously avoiding the sort of showmanship of the court fey or blurs of speed, opting for a casual stroll into the wide-open desert.

Once he was no longer near them, he glanced down at what his jacket had hidden. The darkness on his shirt made clear that his injury was bleeding again, but he'd successfully covered it with the jacket. The faeries behind him hadn't seen his blood, and his posture gave nothing away. This time, he'd pulled it off, but there was a limit to his skills. If Rika didn't come back soon, he wasn't sure he could manage the growing unease—not without revealing just how injured he was, and an injured Alpha was a quickly replaced Alpha.

Resolutely, Sionnach made his way toward her cave yet again. If she hadn't returned, he'd have to send someone to find her.

When he arrived, he found Rika and Jayce on the far side of the cave. From the look of it, they had only just returned. She dropped her bag to the floor, and he felt like a pressure in his chest vanished.

"She returns," he murmured.

"Sionnach." Rika let go of Jayce's hand and turned to look

over her shoulder at him. Her expression was as unreadable as any court fey, and he thought for a moment at how much she'd changed—and how little. She was never easy to know, but her emotions were usually more accessible to him.

He leaned on the cave wall at the opening, needing it for support as much as falling onto it in relief at the sight of her. Behind him was the bright light of the desert, making him a silhouette, allowing him to hide the pain in his own expression a little longer. "Do you suppose you'll forgive me?"

"Why?"

"Because you're stronger than the rest of us? Because I need your support?"

"You *lied.*" She folded her arms over her chest. "You *tricked* me. You *set me up.*"

"You know better than that, Rika. I *misled,*" he corrected. "I'm horrible, but you knew that years ago."

She sighed. "I'm *not* hap—" The word dried up before she finished it.

"You are too. You can't even finish that word because it's a lie, princess. Faeries can't lie." He shook his head. "You and I both know you're happier than you've been as long as I've known you."

He glanced at Jayce, who was standing silently beside Rika. "Because of *you*, Jayce."

Jayce didn't appear moved, didn't seem to appreciate the lengths Sionnach had gone to in order for him to have the privilege of standing at her side. "You were still wrong."

"By Rika's standards, by mortal standards, I was

abhorrent." Sionnach strode toward them so he was directly in front of Rika; his movements were cautious as much from habit as from injury. Slowly, Sionnach brushed her hair away and cupped her face in his hands. "But you're a stubborn faery, Rika. I needed you alive and involved."

"You manipulated me. You should've told me." Her voice was soft, even as she chastised him, but he heard the acceptance too. Rika understood him; she forgave him and challenged him, pushing him to be better—to be worthy of her friendship. He wasn't. He never would be, but he was grateful that he hadn't lost her. He'd known that it was a risk, but he'd hoped against hope that it would turn out well. She'd needed to be nudged into her rightful place, out of her seclusion and into the bright desert light. He'd been willing to risk a lot to see her happy, to see her ruling over the solitaries in the desert, to have her at his side.

"My word, princess. I'll talk to you next time I have plans to manipulate you." He nodded and kissed her nose in a moment of impertinence. "I'm glad you calmed down and came home. Where were you?"

"Getting help." Rika shoved him away with a small growl. "Solving the problem *you* created for me."

Fear crept over him at her words. There weren't a lot of faeries she could seek out to help her in the desert. "What did you do? Rika?"

"I've sworn fealty." She started to walk past him as if she were utterly unconcerned by her admission.

"You *swore fealty*?" Sionnach grabbed her arm and swung

her back to face him. "How could you do that? After everything he's done. . . ."

"But you left me so few choices."

Sionnach stared at her in horror. He'd arranged everything he could to protect her, and she went to Keenan? He knew his outrage was nowhere near hidden as he asked, "So you gave him an excuse to come to our home? You gave him power over you? How could you do that?"

Chapter 21

Rika stared at Sionnach without expression for several moments. She was certain she was missing something. After decades of knowing the fox faery, she found that she could often learn as much by what he didn't say as what he did. There was more to his upset than worry that she'd let Keenan have an easy and regular influence in the desert. Quietly, she said, "I didn't swear to *him*. I don't trust Keenan."

Expression still wary, Sionnach let go of her and took one step backward. "Who? Which court have you invited here? The High Court is in seclusion. . . . The *Dark Court*?" He stepped farther away and glanced at Jayce, who was leaning against the cave wall. "And you? Why didn't you stop her?"

Jayce shrugged. "I swore it too."

"Are you *mad*?" Sionnach looked from one to the other.

Rika walked away and dropped down on one of the pallets on the cave floor. "I offered my loyalty to *Donia*. She is my queen now. I'm sworn to the Winter Court."

He stopped, glanced out the cave mouth into the desert, and then back at Rika. "Winter can't walk here." He nodded. "The Winter Queen is unable to be here . . . but Keenan fears her."

"Exactly." Rika nodded.

At that, Sionnach came to crouch in front of her. He almost looked meek for a moment. "Oh, princess . . . together we are strong enough. We didn't need her."

"I disagree. I can deal with the solitaries—with or without you—but she gives me peace from him." Rika didn't want to admit her weakness, not even now that she felt like she was finally well and truly free of Keenan. He'd been an obstacle to her peace of mind for almost her entire life.

Keenan is standing in the middle of a path in the middle of a forest. "Don't run from me."

"I want you gone." Ice crystals fall from Rika's eyes with tiny clatters. All around her it's summer, but here, in the small circle nearest her, it's frost-filled.

"I told you. These are the rules. You have to talk to the next mortal I choose."

"No."

"As long as none of them take up the test, you're the Winter Girl." He reaches out to her. "Remember how much you said you loved me? This is what I need from you."

"I hate you." Rika backs up. The ice backs up with her. "I never want to see you again."

He sighs. "Our lives are tied together. You'll never stop *seeing me."*

"Stay. Away. From. Me." She turns and runs into the woods, leaving icy footprints behind her like a trail.

Rika shivered. "I won't have Keenan in my desert. I made decisions to fix it. Now, all we need to do is deal with Maili."

After a moment, Sionnach asked hopefully, "We?"

"Yes, *we.* You're a *fox* faery, Shy. I can't expect you to think like a mortal," she said gently. If she stayed angry every time he was what he was, they'd never have become friends. She knew that, but she'd needed to calm down before she could even speak with him. Yes, she was hurt, but she also realized that she should have been more suspicious of his actions; she'd known him too long to be so blindly trusting. She could simply have asked him what his motives were in helping her to be with Jayce. For all his flaws, Sionnach would never directly lie to her; she simply hadn't been paying close attention.

The fox faery grinned. "Really? We fight together?"

Jayce walked over to stand beside Rika and Sionnach. "Don't get too sure of yourself," he cautioned.

Sionnach shrugged and held out a hand to Rika. "Shall we let them know they have two Alphas now, princess? Be my co-Alpha for real?"

Rika glanced at Jayce.

He shook his head. "Go work. I'd rather you two were on the same side, and I'm fine with a little quiet. The light's great for sketching. . . ."

Rika leaned in and kissed Jayce. Although she'd once been a human too, she didn't always understand him. Maybe it was that they were from different places and times, but the easy way he accepted everything—Sionnach, Donia, Alphas, fealty, faery fights, and faery courts—seemed . . . odd. She hadn't been so calm when she'd discovered the oddities of faeries, but maybe it was easier being an observer than an active participant in this world.

"I trust you," Jayce told her quietly. "And when this whole Alpha bit is resolved, you'll be less tense."

Rika felt Sionnach watching her, knew that he was aware that she wasn't telling Jayce everything. Being Alpha wasn't going to make things easier for her, not really. She'd be busier and have more conflicts to handle.

"I'll be back soon," she promised Jayce.

And then, avoiding eye contact with the faery she'd reprimanded for omitting truths, she walked out into the sunlight.

Sionnach and Rika crossed the desert in silence. Although Rika was trying to look serious, he was grinning. They exchanged looks a couple of times.

Finally, Rika looked at him. "Well?"

"Well, what?" His fox tail flicked behind him.

"What's the plan?"

"Make a point. Establish clarity."

"That's the *whole* plan?" she asked.

"You mean the part where we capture Maili?" Sionnach

nudged her with his shoulder. "And you"—his expression became one of feigned innocence—"'talk' to her?"

"Yeah, *that* part." Rika couldn't help it; she felt better. Keenan was banned from the desert; Jayce was accepting of her obligations; and Sionnach was happy and at her side.

"You talk to her, and then we'll take her before the rest." He scurried over a rocky outcropping, not quite as quickly as he usually would.

"I shouldn't look forward to this," Rika said quietly.

Sionnach paused mid-step and leaped down in front of her with a slight wince. "Princess, the only reason you haven't been Alpha around here is stubbornness. You are what you are."

"Looking forward to a fight is—"

"Perfectly normal. You're a solitary faery. A *strong* one. . . ." He pulled back a fist as if to strike her. "And you've spoken your authority into reality."

He swung. Without pause, she stopped him, capturing and holding his fist in her hand.

"This is your territory, and there's a threat in it." He punched upward with the other hand.

She blocked him again.

Gently, he said, "Just like you defend against me without thought, you will defend them."

"Maili doesn't get that about being Alpha, does she?" Rika glanced at Sionnach. In their mock-fight, his jacket had gaped open. She stared at the dried blood on his shirt and at the fresh blood seeping around it like a flower blossoming. "Shy, you're—"

"Fine." He waved her concern away.

"Maili wouldn't understand, not like we do. We have a duty to them, and with you beside me, we can succeed." He nodded at faeries who had crept out to watch them and pulled his jacket closed again casually. Then, in a low voice he added, "But I think that's what you want to *explain* to her."

Rika shook her head and chastised, "It is, but you need to stop hiding things from me."

"I *am* trying." Sionnach linked his arm with hers. "Come now, princess. Run with me?"

"Where?"

"Let me lead you there, and you can handle the fight."

She nodded, and they raced toward a crevice in two rock walls. Rika knew that he held on to her in part because he was still healing from being stabbed, and that only served to increase her anger at Maili.

Sionnach flashed Rika a smile. "Shall we knock?"

"No." She stepped in front of him and disappeared into the opening.

"*There's* my princess," he said as he followed her into what appeared to be a roofless cavern.

Inside were four faeries, including Maili. Rika wasn't sure how to start. Part of her wanted to simply launch herself at Maili, beat her for her selfishness and the pain she'd caused as a result of it. The rest of her knew that wasn't the answer.

Sionnach whistled, and when the faeries looked his way,

he raised a finger and shook it at them like he was scolding a child. "Stay out of it, or share Maili's sentence." Then he gestured Rika toward Maili. "She's all yours, Rika."

Maili tilted her chin up in a defiant posture. "I don't need help fighting her."

"Pretty to think so," Sionnach muttered. He knew that Rika could handle the disobedient faery even if she wasn't angry, and right now, she was still holding on to both anger and hurt over the situation Maili had caused. The fight could only go one way.

The other three faeries stepped back, and Sionnach nodded at them approvingly before clambering up the side of a rock wall and crouching on a ledge. The solitaries were a fickle lot sometimes. They saw the way the winds shifted, and their allegiance shifted with them. It was a large part of why being an Alpha was difficult.

Maili looked at Sionnach appraisingly.

"It would be best if you left the desert," Rika told her, drawing her attention away from Sionnach. "We're willing to let you go if you leave now."

Maili laughed.

"Go." Rika advanced slowly toward Maili.

"When Keenan comes here, you won't be so—"

"He won't be coming here." Rika spread her feet to give herself better balance. She watched Maili carefully as she added, "Third chance, Maili. Your Alphas direct you to leave."

With a yell, Maili launched herself at Rika. "You are *not*

my Alpha. Neither of you are."

For several moments, Rika and Maili exchanged blows. Rika's punches landed more often than not, but Maili was quick on her feet. Rika was out of practice, but her blows were more forceful than most faeries' strikes. The fight wasn't truly well matched; Rika was steadily pummeling Maili, and when the other faery realized that, she grabbed Rika by the throat.

"Bad idea," Sionnach muttered.

Rika took Maili's legs out from under her. The rebellious faery stumbled and—needing her arms to keep her balance—released Rika's throat.

Promptly, Rika delivered a punch to the stomach.

Maili fell to the ground, legs curled to the side. She attempted to get up, and Rika kicked her before glancing up at Sionnach and nodding.

He looked at the faeries who had been there with Maili. "Spread the word that there will be an assembly today."

As the faeries were departing, Rika yanked Maili to her feet and told her, "This wasn't what I wanted. I asked you to leave before this had to happen."

Sionnach hopped down and applauded. He moved slowly, but he'd often moved at that pace, a heightened cautiousness that faeries often saw as his deliberateness. In that moment, Rika wondered how often it had simply been a ploy to hide injuries he'd sustained.

"Step two," Rika said quietly.

Sionnach smiled and echoed, "Step two."

They escorted Maili to a mining shack on the hill in the same abandoned mining town that Sionnach often called home. After they trussed her up, they left Maili inside the solitary mine cart that was stored in the shack, and closed the door. Then, they waited for the faeries to arrive for their first assembly with their new co-Alphas.

Once the crowd had begun to gather, Sionnach climbed gracefully to the top of a dilapidated porch roof and balanced along the fractured railing as if he were oblivious to all the faeries—except Rika. He looked only at her as the faeries started coming closer. Then, he held out one hand to her.

She walked closer to the building and looked up at him as he stood motionless on the battered wooden railing. "What are you doing?"

He crouched down and held out a second hand. "Helping you up."

With far less grace than he had, she clambered up to stand beside him and took his hand in hers.

"Showmanship," he whispered.

Once she was steady, he released her hand and then hopped up to a higher roof, deftly avoiding a gaping hole that looked like a mess of splinters and glass. Then, he looked back at her.

She didn't hesitate as she reached both hands up this time, and with a relieved smile, he lifted her to stand beside him.

Letting go of one hand, they took another step—together—to stand on the roof.

On the ground behind them, faeries had assembled in silence.

"Rika will be beside me keeping order here," Sionnach said by way of introduction. "As co-Alphas we will be happy to keep you safe, at cost to ourselves."

"We will not forgive betrayals easily," Rika glanced at Sionnach. "We would rather not have to have any betrayals, but if you do . . ."

She released Sionnach's hand, and he hopped down with far more ease than they had ascended, looking animal-graceful, and ambled up the hill to the shack. It was once part of the aboveground mine structure, so there were tracks that began near the door. Sionnach pulled the mine cart out and shoved it onto the tracks. Then, he proceeded to push it down the hill and into the dusty street.

The assembled faeries looked alternately amused and curious, and Rika suspected that they were quite aware of which faery was being pushed into the crowd.

Once the cart was almost in their midst, Rika raised her voice and told the crowd, "I've sworn myself to the Winter Queen in order to keep the Summer King from meddling in our desert. Winter will keep him in check, so Sionnach and I can keep *our* home safe. I surrendered part of my own freedom for you."

Sionnach dumped Maili onto the dusty ground in the middle of the street. He untied her, but she still looked rather bruised and dirty.

"This doesn't mean we will be gentle," Sionnach said.

"Rika is every bit as cruel as I am when our home is threatened."

"Or more," Rika added quietly.

"Perhaps." Sionnach shrugged.

"For betraying your Alphas, Maili, we banish you from our desert until such time as you are judged worthy to return." Rika lowered herself to the edge of the roof, sitting so that her feet were dangling, and then placed her hands on either side of her legs. Pushing off while simultaneously spinning around so as not to injure herself, she came to the ground. It was a bit showy, very gymnastic in the fluidity of it, far more so than Sionnach's graceful dismount, but she figured that if she was going to co-rule the desert, she'd best start acting like it. With that in mind she crouched down and jerked Maili to her feet. "If I thought you could remain here—"

"As your dog?" Maili spat the words, her expression haughty. "No. There are other deserts and—"

"You'll be going somewhere else." Sionnach stepped closer to Rika. "You stabbed me. You brought the Summer King to our desert. You conspired to injure all of us."

"I tried to take power from the weaker faeries, those not fit to hold dominion here." Maili's gaze darted to the faces of the faeries around them, seeking support.

The faeries weren't responding. Some glared at her; some looked sorry for her. A few seemed gleeful.

"There is a correct way to take power: you challenge the Alpha. You do not conspire and endanger those the Alpha protects," Sionnach reminded her and all there. "Challenges are fine; treachery is not."

"You'll be going to the court of the Winter Queen to serve your sentence." Rika shuddered. "You'll be surrounded by the cold. . . ."

Maili looked horrified for a split second, and then she launched herself at Rika.

Sionnach caught her before she could move very far, effectively stopping her forward momentum. It was an awful thing, the cold that she'd be facing, but she'd plotted to take away freedom from solitaries and had struck her Alpha. Her punishment had to be harsh.

Rika moved close enough that Maili could reach her.

Predictably, Maili swung; Rika blocked her punch.

"It'll ache every day," Rika whispered. "You'll beg for it to stop."

"You can't . . ." Maili looked stricken, increasingly panicked.

"You broke mortals for sport after Sionnach told you to stop; you stabbed him; you offered me to Keenan . . . you offered them"—Rika gestured at the faeries in the street—"as pawns to him."

Sionnach tightened his grip on Maili's topknot. "Do any of you want to speak for her? Ask mercy? Offer yourself in her stead? Challenge us?"

The faeries shook their heads, and some said "no."

One of the faeries who was Maili's cohort previously asked, "What terms mercy?"

Rika gave Maili a pleading look, hoping to convey what she couldn't in words without undercutting her own authority and Sionnach's too. If Maili tried to adhere to the terms before her, she could end her punishment sooner; doing so only required humility and admission of wrongdoing. "Listen well to the Winter Queen," Rika urged. "She has the power to set you free. Since she is my regent, I must listen to her decisions. If she decides you are suitably punished, you can come h—"

Maili's snarl cut off Rika's words.

At Sionnach's gesture, several faeries stepped forward and took Maili.

"Take her to the edge of the desert," he said. "Rika's queen will have an escort waiting for her."

And at that, Maili was led away.

Afterward, the faeries slowly broke off into small groups. Some talked; others simply left in silence. They'd seen the punishment that their Alphas would mete out to those who didn't follow the rules, and it was enough incentive for them to fall into order as they'd never before done. No one who was a solitary wanted to be given to a court, and no one who chose a life in the desert wanted to be sent to the Winter Court's abode.

After they had all left, Rika and Sionnach sat on a porch, backs to the battered building, silent and watching the crowd as the sky darkened. A coyote crept across the desert in shadow, and stars blinked to life. There were dozens of things that Rika considered saying, chastisements and compliments, but this wasn't the time. He was her partner, and they'd found ways to set things to rights in their home. She wasn't about to forget that he'd manipulated her, and he wasn't liable to ignore the fact that his co-Alpha was also subject to a queen.

"Are we all right?" he asked softly.

"We will be."

They exchanged a smile and looked out together over their kingdom.

Not long afterward, Rika walked through town alone, letting the faeries see her, making eye contact with them. She smiled; she nodded. She *didn't* stop to chitchat; instead, she walked with an authority that they recognized—the sort of authority she once wore as the Winter Girl, the sort Sionnach had been asking her to exert here for years. She passed the skate park and the club. By then, faeries had gathered and begun to follow her.

Finally, she turned and walked into the open desert. Here were the even less-human-looking faeries; they, too, were watching her. Rika moved purposefully, knowing that by now scores of faeries were trailing her at a distance. They walked, crept, and strolled across the expanse of desert like a mismatched platoon of troops marching to battle.

And I will lead and protect them.

Epilogue

Two Years Later

Rika watched Jayce talk to other students after his class. He didn't know she was visiting; she'd wanted to surprise him. It was a strange feeling, looking at him this way. He seemed to laugh more freely when he was at his university campus, and as she watched him, she wondered if this was where they'd been meant to be all along: him living his normal life, the sort of life she never had, and her learning to let him go.

"He still loves you," a voice said.

She turned to see the faery she'd been friends with longer than Jayce had lived. Sionnach's smile was sad, but he didn't have pity in his eyes.

"I know he does." Rika glanced back at Jayce. "He's not going to be content to stay in a cave in the desert though. He hasn't left me yet, but he doesn't visit much any more. He wants his own family, to travel, more and more things

I can't give him. We talked about it last week again. That's why I came to see him."

"Mortals," Sionnach murmured. "Such confusing creatures."

"Says the faery who can't seem to stop dating them," Rika teased. "What's the latest one's name?"

"I'll let you know after the next party." Sionnach draped his arm over her shoulders.

Together they watched Jayce. He looked older after only two years, and his interests were changing so quickly. He'd been her first relationship in decades; truth be told, he was her first healthy relationship despite her having lived for well over a century. What she'd had with Keenan was a cruel game: he'd merely played a role so he could steal her mortality, and she'd spent years convincing other girls not to love him. Admittedly, the whole thing was because of a *curse*, but that didn't change reality. Jayce, however, had loved her for who she was. Theirs was that innocent first love she'd wanted forever ago. It just took a while to find it.

And the manipulation of a fox faery.

After several more moments of comfortable silence, Sionnach asked, "What are you going to do?"

Rika shook her head. "Miss him, I suspect. Hope he meets a mortal girl who makes him happy."

Sionnach nodded. "Sometimes, their changes are enough to make a faery stop wooing mortals." He shot a sideways glance at her that she pretended not to see and then added, "I think about it, too."

"What?"

"A family," he murmured. "Things are calm now that the courts aren't all in a mess."

"Someday, maybe." She'd grown used to feigning ignorance with him.

Of course, he'd grown just as accustomed to trying to be as blunt as possible without overtly saying what he really intended. "*I* could learn to like living in caves."

"True," she agreed blandly.

He laughed and flicked her with his tail.

"Shy?"

Once he looked at her, she asked, "When you first pushed me toward him, did you have another reason? Aside from luring me out of hiding?"

Sionnach removed his arm from around her shoulders, but that was it. He was silent. More than a minute passed before he answered, "Most foxes mate for life, but sometimes a fox faery has to use a bit of . . . strategy to help his mate get ready for that." He stepped in front of her and looked directly at her. "You were still mourning your mortal life, and I didn't know how to give you what you needed to heal. Then, I saw Jayce. I watched you become more alive, and I knew that what you needed was to be with a mortal, to be the mortal you should've been if Keenan hadn't picked you."

Rika realized that her lips had parted on a gasp. She'd known for a while that Sionnach had feelings for her, but not like this. "But you date mortals. A *lot* of them," she objected.

"I like them, and I got lonely while I was waiting for . . . my plans to work." He looked strangely embarrassed then. "It took ages just to get you to see me as a friend, then finally as my partner as Alpha. If I'd walked up to you years ago and said, 'Hello, do want to have a litter of my kits?' you'd never have let me any closer."

There was no way to argue with that. She wasn't sure if she wanted to run *now*. All she could say was, "You don't do commitments."

"Because I chose my mate a very long time ago," he corrected gently.

"Oh."

He started to step away from her, but she grabbed his arm.

"Wait," she said. "I can't do this now." She took a breath before adding, "Not *now*."

The hurt in his expression was replaced with his familiar mischievous grin. In a falsely solemn tone, he asked, "Tuesday? Or maybe Wednesday? I could wait a bit longer. Really, what's a few days after *decades*?"

Rika shook her head at him, but she was smiling. "And here I'd planned on trying to convince you to . . ."

"To?" he prompted.

"Distract me with your wit and charm," she offered.

"*Just* that?"

And Rika laughed before admitting, "For starters."

"Finally getting started sounds good," he said as he caught her hand in his.

Read on to discover how

WICKED LOVELY

began:

Prologue

The Summer King knelt before her. "Is this what you freely choose, to risk winter's chill?"

She watched him—the boy she'd fallen in love with these past weeks. She'd never dreamed he was something other than human, but now his skin glowed as if flames flickered just under the surface, so strange and beautiful she couldn't look away. "It's what I want."

"You understand that if you are not the one, you'll carry the Winter Queen's chill until the next mortal risks this? And you'll warn her not to trust me?" He paused, glancing at her with pain in his eyes.

She nodded.

"If she refuses me, you will tell the next girl and the next"—he moved closer—"and not until one accepts, will you be free of the cold."

"I do understand." She smiled as reassuringly as she could, and then she walked over to the hawthorn bush.

The leaves brushed against her arms as she bent down and reached under it.

Her finger wrapped around the Winter Queen's staff. It was a plain thing, worn as if countless hands had clenched the wood. It was those hands, those other girls who'd stood where she now did, she didn't want to think about.

She stood, hopeful and afraid.

Behind her, he moved closer. The rustling of trees grew almost deafening. The brightness from his skin, his hair, intensified. Her shadow fell on the ground in front of her.

He whispered, "Please. Let her be the one. . . ."

She held the Winter Queen's staff—and hoped. For a moment she even believed, but then ice pierced her, filled her like shards of glass in her veins.

She screamed his name: "Keenan!"

She stumbled toward him, but he walked away, no longer glowing, no longer looking at her.

Then she was alone—with only a wolf for companionship—waiting to tell the next girl what a folly it was to love him, to trust him.

CHAPTER 1

SEERS, or Men of the SECOND SIGHT, . . . have very terrifying Encounters with [the FAIRIES, they call Sleagh Maith, or the Good People].

—The Secret Commonwealth by Robert Kirk and Andrew Lang (1893)

"Four-ball, side pocket." Aislinn pushed the cue forward with a short, quick thrust; the ball dropped into the pocket with a satisfying clack.

Her playing partner, Denny, motioned toward a harder shot, a bank shot.

She rolled her eyes. "What? You in a hurry?"

He pointed with the cue.

"Right." *Focus and control, that's what it's all about.* She sank the two.

He nodded once, as close as he got to praise.

Aislinn circled the table, paused, and chalked the cue. Around her the cracks of balls colliding, low laughter, even the endless stream of country and blues from the jukebox kept her grounded in the real world: the human world, the *safe* world. It wasn't the only world, no matter how much Aislinn wanted it to be. But it hid the other world—the ugly one—for brief moments.

"Three, corner pocket." She sighted down the cue. It was a good shot.

Focus. Control.

Then she felt it: warm air on her skin. A faery, its too-hot breath on her neck, sniffed her hair. His pointed chin pressed against her skin. All the focus in the world didn't make Pointy-Face's attention tolerable.

She scratched: the only ball that dropped was the cue ball.

Denny took the ball in hand. "What was that?"

"Weak-assed?" She forced a smile, looking at Denny, at the table, anywhere but at the horde coming in the door. Even when she looked away, she heard them: laughing and squealing, gnashing teeth and beating wings, a cacophony she couldn't escape. They were out in droves now, freer somehow as evening fell, invading her space, ending any chance of the peace she'd sought.

Denny didn't stare at her, didn't ask hard questions. He just motioned for her to step away from the table and called out, "Gracie, play something for Ash."

At the jukebox Grace keyed in one of the few not-country-or-blues songs: Limp Bizkit's "Break Stuff."

As the oddly comforting lyrics in that gravelly voice took off, building to the inevitable stomach-tightening rage, Aislinn smiled. *If I could let go like that, let the years of aggression spill out onto the fey . . .* She slid her hand over the smooth wood of the cue, watching Pointy-Face gyrate beside Grace. *I'd start with him. Right here, right now.* She bit her lip. Of course, everyone would think she was utterly mad if she started swinging her cue at invisible bodies, everyone but the fey.

Before the song was over, Denny had cleared the table.

"Nice." Aislinn walked over to the wall rack and slid the cue back into an empty spot. Behind her, Pointy-Face giggled—high and shrill—and tore out a couple strands of her hair.

"Rack 'em again?" But Denny's tone said what he didn't: that he knew the answer before he asked. He didn't know why, but he could read the signs.

Pointy-Face slid the strands of her hair over his face.

Aislinn cleared her throat. "Rain check?"

"Sure." Denny began disassembling his cue. The regulars never commented on her odd mood swings or unexplainable habits.

She walked away from the table, murmuring good-byes as she went, consciously not staring at the faeries. They moved balls out of line, bumped into people—anything to cause trouble—but they hadn't stepped in her path tonight, not yet. At the table nearest the door, she paused. "I'm out of here."

One of the guys straightened up from a pretty combination shot. He rubbed his goatee, stroking the gray-shot hair. "Cinderella time?"

"You know how it is—got to get home before the shoe falls off." She lifted her foot, clad in a battered tennis shoe. "No sense tempting any princes."

He snorted and turned back to the table.

A doe-eyed faery eased across the room; bone-thin with too many joints, she was vulgar and gorgeous all at once. Her eyes were far too large for her face, giving her a startled look. Combined with an emaciated body, those eyes made her seem vulnerable, innocent. She wasn't.

None of them are.

The woman at the table beside Aislinn flicked a long ash into an already overflowing ashtray. "See you next weekend."

Aislinn nodded, too tense to answer.

In a blurringly quick move, Doe-Eyes flicked a thin blue tongue out at a cloven-hoofed faery. The faery stepped back, but a trail of blood already dripped down his hollowed cheeks. Doe-Eyes giggled.

Aislinn bit her lip, hard, and lifted a hand in a last half wave to Denny. *Focus.* She fought to keep her steps even, calm: everything she wasn't feeling inside.

She stepped outside, lips firmly shut against dangerous words. She wanted to speak, to tell the fey to leave so she didn't have to, but she couldn't. *Ever.* If she did, they'd know her secret: they'd know she could see them.

The only way to survive was to keep that secret; Grams taught her that rule before she could even write her name: *Keep your head down and your mouth closed.* It felt wrong to have to hide, but if she even hinted at such a rebellious idea, Grams would have her in lockdown—homeschooled, no pool halls, no parties, no freedom, no Seth. She'd spent enough time in that situation during middle school.

Never again.

So—rage in check—Aislinn headed downtown, toward the relative safety of iron bars and steel doors. Whether in its base form or altered into the purer form of steel, iron was poisonous to fey and thus gloriously comforting to her. Despite the faeries that walked her streets, Huntsdale was home. She'd visited Pittsburgh, walked around D.C., explored Atlanta. They were nice enough, but they were too thriving, too alive, too filled with parks and trees. Huntsdale wasn't thriving. It hadn't been for years. That meant the fey didn't thrive here either.

Revelry rang from most of the alcoves and alleys she passed, but it wasn't ever as bad as the thronging choke of faeries that cavorted on the Mall in D.C. or at the Botanical Gardens in Pittsburgh. She tried to comfort herself with that thought as she walked. There were less fey here—less people, too.

Less is good.

The streets weren't empty: people went about their business, shopping, walking, laughing. It was easier for them: they didn't see the blue faery who had cornered several winged fey behind a dirty window; they never saw the faeries with lions' manes racing across power lines, tumbling over one another, landing on a towering woman with angled teeth.

To be so blind... It was a wish Aislinn had held in secret her whole life. But wishing didn't change what *was*. And even if she could somehow stop seeing the fey, a person can't un-know the truth.

She tucked her hands in her pockets and kept walking, past the mother with her obviously exhausted children, past shop windows with frost creeping over them, past the frozen gray sludge all along the street. She shivered. The seemingly endless winter had already begun.

She'd passed the corner of Harper and Third—*almost there*—when *they* stepped out of an alley: the same two faeries who'd followed her almost every day the past two weeks. The girl had long white hair, streaming out like spirals of smoke. Her lips were blue—not lipstick blue, but corpse blue. She wore a faded brown leather skirt stitched with thick cords. Beside her was a huge white wolf that she'd alternately lean on or ride. When the other faery touched her, steam rose from her skin. She bared her teeth at him, shoved him, slapped him: he did nothing but smile.

And he was devastating when he did. He glowed faintly all the time, as if hot coals burned inside him. His collar-length hair shimmered like strands of copper that would slice her skin if Aislinn were to slide her fingers through it—not that she would. Even if he were truly human, he wouldn't be her type—tan and too beautiful to touch, walking with a swagger that said he knew exactly how attractive he was. He moved as if he were in charge of everyone and everything, seeming taller for it. But he wasn't really that tall—not as tall as the bone-girls by the river or the strange tree-bark men that roamed the city. He was almost average in size, only a head taller than she was.

Whenever he came near, she could smell wildflowers, could hear the rustle of willow branches, as if she were sitting by a pond on one of those rare summer days: a taste of midsummer in the start of the frigid fall. And she wanted to keep that taste, bask in it, roll in it until the warmth soaked into her very skin. It terrified her, the almost irresistible urge to get closer to him, to get closer to any of the fey. *He* terrified her.

Aislinn walked a little faster, not running, but faster. *Don't run.* If she ran, they'd chase: faeries always gave chase.

She ducked inside The Comix Connexion. She felt safer among the rows of unpainted wooden bins that lined the shop. *My space.*

Every night she'd slipped away from them, hiding until they passed, waiting until they were out of sight. Sometimes it took a few tries, but so far it had worked.

She waited inside Comix, hoping they hadn't seen.

Then he walked in—wearing a glamour, hiding that glow, passing for human—visible to everyone.

That's new. And new wasn't good, not where the fey were concerned. Faeries walked past her—past everyone—daily, invisible and impossible to hear unless they willed it. The really strong ones, those that could venture further into the city, could weave a glamour—faery manipulation—to hide in plain sight as humans. They frightened her more than the others.

This faery was even worse: he had donned a glamour between one step and the next, becoming suddenly visible, as if revealing himself didn't matter at all.

He stopped at the counter and talked to Eddy—leaning close to be heard over the music that blared from the speakers in the corners.

Eddy glanced her way, and then back at the faery. He said her name. She saw it, even though she couldn't hear it.

No.

The faery started walking toward her, smiling, looking for all the world like one of her wealthier classmates.

She turned away and picked up an old issue of *Nightmares and Fairy Tales*. She clutched it, hoping her hands weren't shaking.

"Aislinn, right?" Faery-boy was beside her, his arm against hers, far too close. He glanced down at the comic, smiling wryly. "Is that any good?"

She stepped back and slowly looked him over. If he was trying to pass for a human she'd want to talk to, he'd failed. From the hems of his faded jeans to his heavy wool coat, he was too uptown. He'd dulled his copper hair to sandy-blond, hidden that strange rustle of summer, but even in his human glamour, he was too pretty to be real.

"Not interested." She slid the comic back in place and walked down the next aisle, trying to keep the fear at bay, and failing.

He followed, steady and too close.

She didn't think he'd hurt her, not here, not in public. For all their flaws, the fey seemed to be better behaved when they wore human faces. Maybe it was fear of the steel bars in human jails. It didn't really matter why: what mattered was that it was a rule they seemed to follow.

But when Aislinn glanced at him, she still wanted to run. He was like one of the big cats in the zoo—stalking its prey from across a ravine.

Deadgirl waited at the front of the shop, invisible, seated on her wolf's back. She had a pensive look on her face, eyes shimmering like an oil slick—strange glints of color in a black puddle.

Don't stare at invisible faeries, Rule #3. Aislinn glanced back down at the bin in front of her calmly, as if she'd been doing nothing more than gazing around the store.

"I'm meeting some people for coffee." Faery-boy moved closer. "You want to come?"

"No." She stepped sideways, putting more distance between them. She swallowed, but it didn't help how dry her mouth was, how terrified and tempted she felt.

He followed. "Some other night."

It wasn't a question, not really. Aislinn shook her head. "Actually, no."

"She already immune to your charms, Keenan?" Deadgirl called out. Her voice was lilting, but there was a harsh edge under the words. "Smart girl."

Aislinn didn't reply: Deadgirl wasn't visible. *Don't*

answer invisible faeries, Rule #2.

He didn't answer her, either, didn't even glance her way. "Can I text you? E-mail? Something?"

"No." Her voice was rough. Her mouth was dry. She swallowed. Her tongue stuck to the roof of her mouth, making a soft clicking noise when she tried to speak. "I'm not interested at all."

But she was.

She hated herself for it, but the closer he stood to her, the more she wanted to say *yes, yes, please yes* to whatever he wanted. She wouldn't, couldn't.

He pulled a piece of paper from his pocket and scrawled something on it. "Here's mine. When you change your mind . . ."

"I won't." She took it—trying not to let her fingers too near his skin, afraid the contact would somehow make it worse—and shoved it in her pocket. *Passive resistance,* that was what Grams would counsel. *Just get through it and get away.*

Eddy was watching her; Deadgirl was watching her.

Faery-boy leaned closer and whispered, "I'd really like to get to know you. . . ." He sniffed her like he really was some sort of animal, no different than the less-human-looking ones. "Really."

And that would be Rule #1: Don't ever attract faeries' attention. Aislinn almost tripped trying to get away—from him and from her own inexplicable urge to give in. She did stumble in the doorway when Deadgirl whispered, "Run while you can."

* * *

Keenan watched Aislinn leave. She didn't really run, but she wanted to. He could feel it, her fear, like the thrumming heart of a startled animal. Mortals didn't usually run from him, especially girls: only one had ever done so in all the years he'd played this game.

This one, though, she was afraid. Her already-pale skin blanched when he reached out to her, making her look like a wraith framed by her straight blue-black hair. *Delicate.* It made her seem more vulnerable, easier to approach. Or maybe that was just because she was so slight. He imagined he could tuck her head under his chin and fit her whole body in the spare fold of his coat. *Perfect.* She'd need some guidance on attire—replace the common clothes she seemed to prefer, add a few bits of jewelry—but that was inevitable these days. At least she had long hair.

She'd be a refreshing challenge, too, in strange control of her emotions. Most of the girls he'd picked were so fiery, so volatile. Once he'd thought that was a good indicator—Summer Queen, fiery passion. It had made sense.

Donia interrupted his thoughts: "I don't think she likes you."

"So?"

Donia pursed her blue lips—the only spot of color in her cold, white face.

If he studied her, he could find proof of the changes in her—the blond hair faded to the white of a snow squall, the pallor that made her lips seem so blue—but she was still as beautiful as she had been when she'd taken over as the Winter Girl. *Beautiful, but not mine, not like Aislinn will be.*

"Keenan," Donia snapped, a cloud of frigid air slipping out with her voice. "She doesn't like you."

"She will." He stepped outside and shook off the glamour. Then he said the words that'd sealed so many mortal girls' fates. "I've dreamed about her. She's the one."

And with that Aislinn's mortality began to fade. Unless she became the Winter Girl, she was his now—for better or for worse.

Don't miss Melissa Marr's bestselling series

WICKED LOVELY

Like Wicked Lovely on Facebook
www.facebook.com/wickedlovelyofficial

HARPER

An Imprint of HarperCollins*Publishers*